Tzu Kingdom
Stanley's Discovery

Karen Chilvers & Gill Eastgate

Britain's Next
BESTSELLER

First published in 2016 by:

Britain's Next Bestseller
An imprint of Live It Publishing
27 Old Gloucester Road
London, United Kingdom.
WC1N 3AX

www.britainsnextbestseller.co.uk

ISBN 978-1-910565872

For Lola & Phoebe

Supporter List

6VT Youth Café, Abby, Abby & Mum, Abi Stevens, Adam Prior, Alexander Wells, Alison Fulcher, Amelia Lyon, Andrea Pereira, Andrew Page, Angus, Annabel Robb, Annabelle, Archie James Brown, Arron, Aulay, Ava, Ava Valentina Aspinell, Bailey & Wrigley, Bentley Boo, Bertie, Betsy Dougan. Binkybear Frausto, Bob Barr, Bodie, Boo Boo, Gypsy, Nancy & Quincy, Bricktop, Bunnie Boing, Calum & Anna Mackenzie, Carol Negus, Carole, Caron Lindsay, Chris, Chris Miller, Christian & Claire Kim, Christine Wells, Coconut, Coffee, Cooper Dogley, Courtney , Cricketbug, Custard Long-Legs, Danni & Coco Pereyda, David Kendall, Debra Robinson, Deneena & Beckham Davis, Dominic Phillip Naylor, Doreen Price, EC Morrison, Eden, Edinburgh City Youth Café, Ella & Freya Main, Ella Mae, Ella, Patrick John Ellis & Freya Turnbull, Emilie, Emma, Eva Grace Lebow, Felicity Nola Smith, Findlay Benedict McMillan, Finley & Sonny Newstead, Finley Pollard, Flynn Luca Aspinell, Freddie Suett, Freya Wright, Frisbee & Fritter Bradley, Gabriella Pepper, Gayathri Chakravarthy, Grace Harriet Brown, Hairatio (Hairry) Mindblower, Hamish John Roderick McMillan, Hannah Mclean, Harrison, Harry Rovai, Helen Willson, Hollie, Sophie & Arron, Holly Erin Lewis, Holly Lawrence, Honey Badger & Frisky, Dingo, Ian Edmonds, Ian Greig, Isla & Fraser, Jacob Robb, Jake Michael Aspinell, Jakub Price, James Lappin, James Sapwell, Jane Paterson, Jazz, Jenni, Jiro, John Chilvers, Joseph Daniel Gorski, Joseph Robert Corsan, Joyce Payne, Julian Lucioli-Brown, June Spencer, Juniper

Rose McMillan, Kaia, Rosie & Lilly, Katie Morton, Katie Ray, Kay Davidson, Kelso, Kevin Mcnamara, Kiki, Kim Smith, Laura Stewart, Lennie Masterton, Leo, Leon & Maddison Mcculloch, Lil Aubie, Limsey & Pickles, Linda Baxter, Linda Edmonds, Linda Mascot, Linda Price, Lola Pops Holt, Lolabean, Lottie, Louis Battenberg, Lucia Robles, MAC BT, Maggie May, Maisie, Maria (Picklesbottom) Stevens, Marilyn Roden, Mary Kaye & Tuxie, Mary, Cameron Amelia & Noah, Mason, Mathilda & Millicent Mortimer, Matia Gilmou, Matt Lee, Maureen Eastgate, Max, Mia & Pippin, Mike Jones, Mikie Riddell, Mimi & Isabel, Molly, Molly Lolly, My friend Brian, Myra Harman, Neil Mitchell, Noah, Nutshell Studios, Oliver George Crozier, Olivia & Sophia, Otis Ash McMillan, Percy Bertie, Peter & Joyce Crane, Phoenix, Pickles, Poppy & Betty, Ray Foreman, Reice Michael Jupiter, Rhona & Andrew, Riley George Moore, Robbie, Rocky, Rod & Janet Mcmillan, Rosanna Wells, Roxy Tilling, Ruaridh & Freya, Ruben Sanchez, Saffron, Samuel Robb, Samurai Jones, Sandie, Sandra Read, Sarah HH, Sarah Ormrod, Scarlett Quance Anderson, Seamus, Seth, Siya Tyler, Skye Fulcher, Skyepie Horne, Skylar Horne, Sofia, Solomon Hugh McMillan, Sophie & Josh Brown, Stephen Price, Tanya Tarantino, Taylor & Jack, Teddy Stevens, Thomas Philip Crozier, Thomas Spearman, Tiana Juliet Corsan, Tiger, Tim Prater, Tiny_ Boy, Trey Richardson, Tricky Catz, Vanessa, Jay & Future Grand-Tots, Vikki Kavanagh, Wallydog, Willow Tomlin and Zeus.

Chapter 1

STANLEY the vanilla sugar coloured Shih Tzu looked out over his charming edge-of-city garden and, although he was a super happy dog, he sighed loudly to himself as he pondered his problem.

'I love Mama and Daddy' thought the little dog 'but I really wish I had some Tzu friends'.

He truly did love them too, from his cute little nose to the tips of his toes, however he couldn't actually talk to them about "tzu stuff". Stanley constantly wondered if his tail was too fluffy or not fluffy enough, whether his nose was in the right place and if his paws were quite as big as they looked from where he was.

He tried his best to discuss his concerns, although it was as if he talked a different language to them. Whatever he said, all they heard were woofs and barks and, although they cuddled him and laughed and said he was "cute", a "good boy" and their "special soldier", it didn't actually get to the heart of the matter. All these things were wonderful, of course, but then again, he was a deep thinking and clever dog who needed, well, something extra.

'Nevertheless, I'm lucky,' he thought. Stanley had heard stories of other dogs that didn't have a bed of their own in every room in the house, didn't get fed every day and didn't have any toys. He was sad for them and he knew he was "one of the lucky ones" as Mama often told him when she hugged him because she had heard about one less fortunate.

Stanley loved his garden – it was his magical place and he looked at it and smiled. 'This is so beautiful' he mused as he checked everything was as it should be. The coloured lights in the trees were being charged by the winter sun so they would twinkle in the garden when it got dark, the robins were singing in the trees, the trickly waterfall was trickling water in to the pond and the winter flowers were all of a sparkle, plus there was a Shih Tzu tail disappearing into the big tree.....

WHAT?

A Shih Tzu tail?

In his garden?

The little tzu shook his head and looked again.

He ran down the rustic wooden steps as fast as his little furry legs could take him to the biggest - and oldest - tree in the garden but there was nothing to be seen – and certainly not a Shih Tzu! 'I imagined it... me and my wishful thinking!' he chuckled to himself.

Stanley's ears pricked up....Mama was calling him and he dashed back inside...running back up the steps two at a time wondering what delicious dinner he would get today!

But the thing is, he certainly had seen that very thing he wanted to see....attached to another wonderful little Shih Tzu and it would change his life forever.

Chapter 2

THE next day, Stanley woke up to see Mama looking out of the bedroom window in a very excited manner.

"It's snowing poppet!" she said in her lovely warm Scottish way "everything is covered in a snow blanket! Even the Castle!"

He eyed her suspiciously on this occasion. He trusted Mama with every inch of his tzu being, although he was sure that it had snowed last year when he was still a puppy and he definitely didn't remember snow being very "blanketty". He did remember falling over in it and being very cold and frightened until Daddy picked him up and tucked him inside his roomy duffle coat for warmth. A blanket, as far as Stanley was concerned, should be cosy and snuggly and should not be made of snowflakes.

"Shall we go out and play Stanners cutie pie?" she asked him. "You can be all as brave as a lion now you're a big boy!"

Now, one of this little dog's favourite things was sleeping and he wasn't very sure that getting out of his comfy bed and going to play in the freezing cold outdoors was something he seriously wanted to do however Mama was so excited that he didn't feel like he had a choice somehow. Daddy was at work, so he couldn't send him and he wasn't going to let her play all by herself!

He jumped down out of the big bed. Well, he did have a lovely new warm winter coat to wear and he wasn't a puppy any more...he was a grown up dog and as brave as a lion...snow play it was!

Stanley and Mama went downstairs and wrapped up in their warm coats, hats and scarves. There was talk of building a snowdog and making snow angels and it all sounded an awful lot of fun. They ran out in to the garden and played with snowballs for a while, laughed at their foot and paw prints and wrote their names in the snow. Mama drew an enormous love heart around their names to show how much she loved him. Then, Mama said that they had better put some seed and fat balls out for the wild birds that so excited him and he ran around her feet whilst she got the dispensers.

"Stanley, you're going to trip me up doing that!" she said so, to keep her safe from falling over, he wandered down to the big tree whilst she filled up the feeders with bird seed.

Only then did he realise just how cold his toes were and he started to wish he had something warm on his paws.

"Here..." woofed a voice with a Canadian accent "try these on for size."

Stanley could not believe his eyes! Stood before him stood a cappuccino coloured dog that looked almost exactly like him, except a little smaller and a little shorter with gigantic mocha coloured eyes and the longest, silkiest, cream coloured ears he had ever seen.

In a flash, he realised that this was the owner of the tzu tail he had seen yesterday. What's more, she was holding out two pairs of shiny red boots.

"Pardon me? Hello?" muttered Stanley. He was so confused.

"Try them on little fella, I think they'll fit you and you will heat up in no time...but dry your paws with this first." She spoke in a soft and kindly voice as she passed him a fluffy towel with maple leaves embroidered in the corners. It smelt yummy, of raspberry flavoured shampoo and syrup!

She was so kind, he did just as he was told, feeling pretty sure he would feel warmer in the paw department if he did so.

"I'm Coffee, Queen of Tzus" she said, as she took a small notebook and pencil out from her jumper pocket, "you're....Stanley...yes?" she said peering over the top of a half-moon pair of reading glasses.

"Yes, I am Stanley the Shih Tzu....You're....erm.... Queen Tzu?" he said, inquisitively and a bit scared. He'd never been introduced to royalty before.

Queen Coffee nodded and smiled, deftly ticked Stanley's name off of a list and made a few notes before neatly slipping her gold rimmed glasses, notebook and pencil back in her pocket and folding up the towel in her paws.

"Well, welcome to Tzu Kingdom! You are our newest friend!"

The Queen of Tzus kissed little Stanley on both of his long ears and the top of his nose.

"Must dash sweetie, I've lots more tzus to check in today. Now, King Bailey Tzu is having a welcome reception on Friday at 6pm. Be here — promptly - at the tree wearing your best "bib and tucker". Someone from the welcome party will be here to greet you and take you through to Tzu Kingdom."

He shook his head, barely able to take it all in. When he opened his eyes, Queen Coffee was nowhere to be seen.

Chapter 3

WELL, now Stanley didn't know if he'd imagined the whole thing in all the dizziness of running about in the snow with Mama. He ran back towards the house, telling her about everything that had just happened to him; about Queen Coffee of Tzus with her little notebook, Tzu Kingdom, the kiss on his nose and that he had been invited to a party on Friday night. As usual, it simply came out as a series of excited woofs and barks.

"Good boy, Stanners" said Mama as she finished putting the bird food away in its tin. "Come on, let's go inside and dry off." She smiled and laughed at him. "You are excited little one" and she ruffled the top of his fluffy head and walked toward the back door.

"Mama mama...do you love my new boots" he said as they got to the steps. He looked down at his paws but noticed that they had gone!

Where are my boots? He panicked.

He ran back and glanced down to the bottom of the garden where the big tree was. Out of the corner of his eye he saw two little giggling fairies pick up his red boots and wink at him as they tucked the boots back out of sight. Stanley blinked, gave a little giggle too, louder and deeper than the fairy giggles and waved them good day.

He followed Mama back in to the house and she grabbed his fluffy white towel off the radiator and began drying his little furry white body dry and then he smelt it on himself — raspberries and syrup!

"Oh my goodness! Queen Coffee and Tzu Kingdom and the Friday night party...it's all true..." he said quietly to himself, knowing that, just as he had hoped, there was excitement ahead with some new tzu friends.

Chapter 4

FRIDAY took forever and ever to arrive and when it did, every second seemed like a whole minute and every minute seemed to take an hour to tick by on the clock in the hall. It ticked just as slowly on the clock in the kitchen. It ticked even slower on the clock on the mantelpiece.

At five to six, Stanley woofed to Mama to go out the garden and ran straight down to the tree and waited patiently for a tzu pal. He had followed Queen Coffee's dress code instructions and was wearing his smartest tartan waistcoat and a bow tie. He hoped this was what she meant by his best "bib and tucker" because he already knew from experience that following the Queen's instructions was a wise thing to do.

Time didn't go any faster in the garden either.

He waited patiently, trying not to blink in case he missed his escort but he couldn't keep his eyes open any more and he blinked several times, making the world before him go all blurry. He was hoping and hoping that he hadn't imagined it after all. He shook his head and there before him was a small black and white curly furred tzu, wearing a dark blue beany hat.

"Hey, Stan the Man? Pleased to meet you pal, I'm Paddy Boo the Shih Tzu. Top model. Coolest dog on the planet. Fearless protector of family. I sleep with a pink bunny toy and I'm proud of who I am!"

For a second, Stanley didn't know what to say and

9

they looked at each other in silence. Then he couldn't hold it any longer and he burst out laughing!

"What's funny fella?" asked Paddy but he was laughing too!

"Come on pal, let's be getting to the party" said the coolest dog on the planet and grabbed Stan's paw. "Hold tight, you might get dizzy the first time we go through the doors, you'll burp for sure, although you'll soon get used to it."

Both boys knew, somewhere inside, that they were going to be the best of friends.

Paddy barked loudly and firmly and, right in front of their eyes, a rainbow coloured door appeared, a golden handle turned and there were two giggling fairies holding back a tiny half door each. Stan recognised them as the same ones who had tidied away his boots for safety.

"We'll never get through there Paddy," said a startled Stanley, looking at the tiny door.

"Hold on to your tail pal!" said Paddy, smiling.

As if by magic, well definitely magic, Stanley now found himself on the other side of the doors in the most beautiful land, dizzy and thankfully still holding Paddy's paw.

They both burped.

"Come on Stan....follow me!"

He followed his new pal as they ran through a corridor. He heard music and laughter that got louder the closer they got.

The first thing that hit Stanley was the smell; it was divine, reminiscent of Granny's kitchen at Christmas — turkey, roast beef and bacon. Oh my goodness he was in heaven!

He glanced up above, gravy and milk bone garlands decked out the room from corner to corner. He looked back down at the tables that were set with bowls of biscuits and brightly coloured napkins lay to the side (presumably for wiping ones beard after eating thought Stanley, thinking perhaps that his current method of wiping his beard on the carpet was clearly not the best). In the centre of each table were enormous displays of roses made from bacon rashers — they looked delicious and Stanley couldn't wait to have a sniff.

He could hardly take it in but the surprises just kept on coming! To his right he could see an ice rink and a snow covered ski slope. To his left was a tropical beach with tzus playing in the sand and — no, surely not — but yes it was... a trio of surfing tzus!

"What you think then? Is it what you expected?" enquired Paddy. Stan was woofless.

Before he could even start on the food, a tzu stood on a chair and made an announcement over the loudspeaker.

"Tzus! Grab your boots and your partners...let's get this party started with a "Paw Stomp"!"

Stan was almost deafened by the screams of excitement as all the tzus started running in all directions, pulling on cowboy boots and arranging themselves in parallel lines covering the whole dance floor.

"Paddy, what's going on?" he said.

"It's every tzu's favourite dance this one Stanley. Never mind the *"Furry Tail Fandango"* or the *"Shih Tzu Shuffle"* - it's the *"Paw Stomp"*! We have to grab our boots - yours will be over here somewhere... quick...let's be getting them on. What's even better is that Peekaboo the Shih Tzu is here tonight to call the moves and she is the best dancer in all of Tzu Kingdom!"

Paddy was right, Stan loved the Paw Stomp and he tried his best to keep up the whole way through as he shook his fluffy booty with gusto. It didn't matter who you partnered with — it was a dance for friends - and Paddy and him stuck together as the dance went

11

back and forth — **STOMP STOMP** — and side to side — **STOMP STOMP** — and round in a circle and jumped — **STOMP STOMP STOMP STOMP!**

The final stomps ended and all the dancing tzus collapsed in a heap together, laughing raucously with exhaustion!

The music changed pace. "Time for a **Shih Tzu Shuffle**" said Peekaboo. Everyone went off to change their shoes.

"I'm going to find someone special for this one, you don't mind do you?" said Paddy "there's plenty of girlies around for a slow dance" he said over his shoulder as he headed across the room.

Stanley didn't mind. Paddy deserved a dance and he waved as he noticed him glide back on to the dance floor with a glossy coated black tzu, holding paws. The lights changed to beautiful colours and the music kicked in. Stanley recognised it as one of the songs that Mama tried her hardest to sing to him at home, whilst she twirled him around giggling in her arms in the lounge on their cosy evenings together. He could feel his body start to sway and, for a second, he felt a little bit sad and a little silly. He would love to get up and dance, just not on his own.

He headed off to the buffet — he hadn't had a chance to have anything to eat with so much excitement. There was definitely a bacon rose with his name on it and also, he heard, there was a gravy fountain to try too!

He happily munched away at all the wonderful treats then, through the dancing, music and hullabaloo he heard a familiar voice — Queen Coffee — and he spun round to face her.

"Stanley, how lovely to see you sweetie, may I introduce the King of Tzus? Bailey, Bailey...this is Stanley, the young vanilla tzu I was telling you about."

He gulped at the thought of meeting more royalty and

not just anyone....but the King! When he met Coffee he didn't know who she was at first however this time he was all too aware. It felt different and he was ever so scared.

In fact, he was trembling all over at the thought of a big, important tzu with a crown and a robe. There was no need though because Bailey, King of Tzus, was the happiest and friendliest of dogs. Everyone loved their King and he loved every one of them back even more and you could see why as an elder, yet spritely, white & black tzu danced in to view and over to where Stanley stood, mesmerised.

"Stanley...welcome!" said the King as he flung his paws around him as if meeting his bestest friend. He was tiny and his big smile showed none of the airs and graces you might expect from one so mighty in status. For sure, he had his paws on the floor. He didn't look like he'd be comfortable wearing a crown and that, if he did have a robe, he'd probably lose it in the park.

"Welcome, welcome young fella! You are the handsome one aren't you?! Have you had plenty to eat? Have you tried the New York sausages? Would you care for some cheese? Can we get you a drink?"

"Questions, questions, questions my beloved!" Coffee interrupted her husband in her usual calm manner "The young man can help himself to the buffet, he's more than capable!"

"In that case, let's all dance!" said King Bailey and, with a shimmy and a shake, led all the tzus back on to the dance floor for a lively Furry Tail Fandango, scooping Stanley up on his way.

Wow. What a King!

Chapter 5

THE welcome party continued until late with singing, dancing and much enjoying of food. Time had gone so painfully slowly earlier in the day, but then again the party seemed to pass by in nanoseconds and Stanley soon found himself in a "tidy team".

Coffee and Bailey had organised everyone in to groups and they were all happily sweeping, washing up and putting the leftovers away for breakfast. Chores didn't seem like chores in Tzu Kingdom and Stanley had been put on sweeping duty with Paddy and Phoebe, the tzu he'd seen him dance the Shih Tzu Shuffle with earlier. He had had a chance to talk to her now and learned that she hailed from New York, wore a smart red biker jacket and made everyone laugh with her funny stories about sidewalks, dog parks and fire hydrants. She was one of the bigger girls and she seemed to want to organise everyone, she was a natural born leader!

Sweeping done, he went to say good night to the Queen and found her in the Chill Out Room putting the finishing touches to the tidying. He also wanted to ask how he was going to get home to Mama and Daddy and explain where he had been all this time. He rather hoped Coffee had a plan for all this.

"Hi sweetie, did you have a good time, did you make some new chums?" she said, plumping up the silken cushions and arranging them in the order of a rainbow.

"Yes thank you my Queen Coffee I have so many tzu friends from all over the world now! I must make a list when I get home so I don't forget anyone! I wondered if you would show me how to get home? Mama and Daddy must be frantic with worry about me, I've been gone ages!"

"Oh sweetie, you must not worry, we will drop you back in your garden at your fairy door just five minutes after you left, they will think you were quickly out doing your necessities in the garden! You must get up to speed on the fairy magic! Paddy will teach you how to open the doors by yourself. He's quite the comedian isn't he?!"

Stanley felt a bit daft not knowing how fairy magic worked, but he was new so he figured this was the best time to find out more about that and Tzu Kingdom in general.

"I love Tzu Kingdom Coffee, but how did it get here?" he said, with his head on one side.

"Sweet pup, I knew you would ask that. You really are wise beyond your years, just like King Bailey in his younger days. I can see a big future ahead for you here my lovely."

Coffee nodded towards the deep, plump pile of cushions she had been tidying and they slumped down in the soft, marshmallowy squishiness so she could deliver a history lesson.

Chapter 6

ABOUT six hundred dog years ago, Shih Tzus only lived in one land a long way from where you live. It was in the Far, Far East and they had lived, played and cuddled there for thousands of dog years before that.

It was a beautiful summer day and they were so happy skipping, jumping and chasing each other about in their palace grounds.

All of a sudden, from absolutely nowhere, a freak storm began. The sun went into hiding and gave way to intense windy rain, black clouds, thunder and lightning. It caught the tzus unaware and they ran for cover and waited for the storm to pass.

The storm stopped as suddenly as it had begun and the gang ventured out of their hiding place — the adult tzus first for safety, ushering the youngsters out when they knew it was safe.

Even though the sturdy tzus were unscathed by the storm, some more delicate creatures were not so fortunate.

As they gathered up their toys, one of the youngest tzus, Leo, heard a faint cry of help. It was coming from the lake. They had never ventured so far before, but now, someone clearly needed their help.

They ran down the grassy slopes as fast as their little legs could go and found fairies of all colours caught in an enormous fishing net, tired, upset and exhausted. They too had been taken by surprise, blown off course by the winds and were now trapped with their intricate wings, and their very lives, in serious peril.

Without even thinking, Leo divided the tzus in to action teams and they all set to work with their nimble paws and delicate teeth, working in pairs to unhook every fairy and his or her tiny wings. The complicated rescue was eventually completed with all fairies free, unhurt and fluttering once again. It had taken hours, in to the night, but the tzus and their teamwork, patience and skill had saved the fairies from perishing.

Leo and his friends wished the fairies well and went back to the palace, pleased to be able to help and proud of how they had all worked together.

The next day, he was surprised to see a small delegation of fairies appear at the gates of their home.

They thanked the tzus once again for saving them from such mortal danger and asked if there was anything they could gift to them. The tzus turned to Leo — after all it had been his long ears that had heard their cries for help.

Leo could only think of one thing after his adventure to the lake…to see the world.

The fairies then decreed that all Shih Tzus could use their fairy door network to visit new lands…shrinking down to squeeze through with fairy magic.

After this, Shih Tzus started to spread out through the world, making new friends and settling in new lands. Nonetheless they missed snuggling up, eating and playing games with each other and soon wished they had somewhere to meet up and this time, they asked the fairies for their help.

The fairies understood and set about setting up a palace within the fairy kingdom where the tzus could meet. They called it Tzu Kingdom on the condition that they would keep it beautiful, they would keep it secret and that they would elect the wisest tzu to be their King or Queen and they would see that it was always used for good.

The tzus accepted this offer and were quick to make Leo their first King for his bravery and leadership qualities. Over the next few years, Leo made Tzu Kingdom what it is today and laid down the foundations for all future Kings and Queens to keep the promise they made to the fairies….a promise that Bailey and I take very seriously indeed and, in time, we will make sure that another Royal Tzu Ruler will uphold.

Stanley loved his history lesson and had loads and loads of questions to ask. He wanted to know what became of King Leo and what good things they did as promised to the fairies when, suddenly, they were interrupted by the thundering of paws and a cacophony of barking. It was Paddy...running helter skelter in to the Chill Out Room, followed by a worried looking Phoebe.

"Queen Coffee" he said, almost completely out of puff..."I need you and King Bailey to help us....there's a baby tzu....and she's in mortal peril..."

Chapter 7

THE keeper of the bar tzus got the stressed out Paddy a drink of milk and a biscuit to steady his nerves as he began to explain what he had seen.

"I had just popped up the Scout Tower with Phoebe for a final look out before home time, when I heard a baby tzu crying. I thought I heard her last week except I wasn't sure." he said.

All the tzus that had stayed late to the party were listening intently to Paddy, all sat around on cushions, with their heads cocked to one side, their eyes brightly alert and their ears raised. The scout tzus were the ones who brought all the important news in because they were responsible for finding new tzus to welcome in to Tzu Kingdom. Coffee, as well as being Queen, was the most experienced scout and she was excellent, she had taught Paddy and his colleagues everything they needed to know to be superb scouts and, despite being young, in truth he was her star student. He'd taken over much of the stewardship of Scout Tower recently as she had other, more queenly responsibilities to worry about and it wasn't seemly for such a regal dog to be scampering up on lookout! Plus, although she kept it to herself, she got a little bit dizzy at height these days so she was glad to start to "hand the telescope" over to Paddy if truth be known.

Paddy the scout continued.

"So I looked through the telescope to where I heard

the cry and she was out, in the cold and dark, on her own. She is so small and skinny I don't think she is being fed properly and, what's worse..." he gulped, "I don't think anyone actually loves her."

A gigantic gasp echoed around Tzu Kingdom. Many tzus had had misfortune such as this in the past, even Bailey himself, so they didn't like to hear of it and it shocked them that any tzu could be unloved.

"We have to do something King Bailey and I don't believe there's a moment to waste."

The Tzu King was pacing up and down, shaking his head and thinking wisely. After a few minutes he spoke.

"You have done excellent work Paddy and I am proud of you."

Paddy stood up straight and puffed out his chest. The King's compliment meant a lot to him.

"I agree. So does my Queen Coffee" he looked at her inquisitively and she nodded, "we have to move her out of the situation — tonight."

"This is a job for the top team — we will need five tzus to mount a rescue like this, using the "coax and sweep" plan. Paddy, you're the scout so you know where we looking. Phoebe, you should go — you two work well together."

Paddy winked at Phoebe, he was rather fond of her — she was more than just a friend. She was a "rescuer" and one of the very best. She was his action girl and he thought she was amazing.

"Phoebe you lead the mission and take rescuers Alice, Pom Pom and Tanner. I know you'll bring her home safe."

"King, there's a problem." said Phoebe, "Tanner has gone home. His family were going on holiday with him and he needed to be back to supervise his basket, food and toys going in to the car. He's just not available for a mission for a couple of weeks — he will

22

be in the car, holidaying in a country cottage, going on long walks where he doesn't know and, well, he can't be missing, not for a moment. We will need a volunteer replacement."

The gathered tzus got incredibly noisy as they all started to discuss who would be the best to go on a rescue mission when amidst the hubbub; a little paw went up in the air.

It was Stanley's.

"Erm, King Bailey, I would be willing to assist. I'm a grown up tzu now and I am as brave as a lion."

Stunned, the tzus looked at the newest little recruit and then, spontaneously, burst in to a round of applause.

"NO!" shouted King Bailey and the room fell immediately silent. "You're too young."

The King wandered off in to the corner and his precious wife, Coffee, followed him.

"Honey, what's the matter? Why are you cross? Are you thinking of Colin? It worked out for him in the end Bailey. He is almost as happy doing what he does now as he would have been as a rescuer."

Bailey nodded, tears in his little eyes. Back in his first year as King of Tzus he had allowed a young tzu to go on a dangerous mission and he was injured in the line of duty. Young Colin had wanted to be a rescuer however his injuries meant he couldn't be and he now worked in the Welcome Room with the Elder Tzus and walked with a limp.

"Yes, he's almost as happy, Coffee, *almost*."

Coffee didn't know what to say when it came to Colin, it genuinely upset Bailey...he blamed himself and he probably always would. But the truth was, the brave dog never blamed Bailey, he knew he took an unnecessary risk and he absolutely loved working with the Elders as part of the welcoming team. He adored it there – Suki with her vast spectacles and books (she taught him to read), Carmen (always knitting him jumpers), Lennon (who was teaching him to play guitar) and Zena (with her amazing collection of hats). They all spoilt him and he loved it, yet Bailey remained defiantly unconvinced.

"Excuse me" said a little voice. It was Phoebe.

"King B, young Stanley really does want to come on the mission and, well, I think with the little tzu-less-fortunate being so young she might be scared. I imagine it would be for the best if a very young tzu came with us to get her or she may run and then, well, we might never be able to get her to safety. He really is brave and I promise I won't let any harm come to him....or the little one."

Coffee smiled at Phoebe. She was a smart, clever and sensible girl.

Bailey paced up and down a little bit more and then, remembering he was their King, he stood as tall as he could and spoke in a firm and commanding voice.

"Stanley Tzu...do you promise to do as you are told on the mission and follow the instructions of the Tzus of Experience?

"Yes I do. I am as brave as a lion and obedient too."

"Paddy, do not let this little one out of your sight and bring him back in one piece. Stanley, you stick with Paddy and do exactly what he tells you. Phoebe, you are leading this mission — you must watch them all."

"Be careful, be brave, be tzu." said the King as he hugged each one of them goodbye.

Chapter 8

PADDY led the team through the fairy door network and right to the garden where he heard the cries of the baby tzu. Once they got close, they realised just how bad things were and how right they were to move in quickly.

She was so little, even for a baby girl, and they watched for a few minutes. She was crying and shivering, her fur was matted and whatever colour she might have been, she was grubby and dirty and several shades of black and grey. Despite all this, she was trying to sing herself happy. It was the saddest sight the team had ever seen, especially the new recruit who had been loved since he was a tiny puppy.

A great big scary woman in a tracksuit came out of the house, holding a bottle of beer and a smelly, burning stick. She swigged from the bottle, shouted at the little dog for crying and pointed at a broken kennel, surrounded by smashed glass and empty tin cans, as she puffed out smoke that nearly made the tzus cough and give themselves away.

The tzus focused on their mission as they hid behind a tree and took their instructions from Phoebe.

"Alice, Pom Pom...you stand by the tree and make sure the fairy door is open as soon as we need it. I shall go halfway to the kennel and keep an eye on you all...Paddy you take Stanley to the kennel and convince the pup to come to Tzu Kingdom. Send Stanley in first because he is young and you stand

27

outside the kennel and keep watch. It's dangerous; she's not chained or trapped so if we move quickly we can get her away swiftly.

"GO GO GO"

The rescuers took up their positions and Stanley ventured in to the kennel.

"Hello little girl, I'm Stanley and my friends and I have come to rescue you and take you somewhere safe."

"Oh, hello, I am safe though. This is my home. But thank you."

She smiled. She had clearly never known anything nice.

"No, sweet little tzu baby, this is not an appropriate home for a Shih Tzu. Home is where you are loved and looked after and cuddled. What is your name?"

"Erm, well Mummy calls me IT or DOG or THAT. She says that when I am grown up I will be Precious once I have a few puppies she can sell. And then she says I can take my chances." She smiled, weakly, as a tear rolled down her whiskers, without her even noticing.

Horrified, Stanley didn't know what to say. She deserved so much better and he knew he could help, although he didn't have enough experience to tell her that there was better than this. He thought about Mama and Daddy and all the fun things they did and he wanted to scoop her up and take her home with him.

Paddy, hearing all this from outside the kennel, could take no more, he had to jump in and help. He appeared at the door and interrupted sharply. This was clearly making him extremely cross.

"Sweetheart, this lady doesn't love you, she's a nasty. She's gonna use you as a puppy machine to make money out of you. A real tzu mother would make sure you were warm and fed, had a squishy bed or three and give you a bath and a brush to keep you beautiful."

"Come with us, we will keep you warm, safe and love you and find you a home where someone worthy of being called your mum will give you a warm bed, lots of love, food and a bath."

The little girl looked at Paddy and Stanley. They were boys and yet their fur was beautiful, bouncy and clean with perfectly manicured nails, clean ears and bright, shiny eyes. She looked down at her dirty paws and long grubby nails and began to cry and cry. Big strong Paddy scooped her up into his soft warm, furry paws and put the crying mess over his shoulder. For a little tzu, he was very strong indeed.

"Trust us darling: Let's get you safe."

They started running towards Pom Pom and Alice at the fairy doors with the sobbing baby clinging on to Paddy. Phoebe joined them on the way. Mission accomplished — almost — they had the one less fortunate and they were taking her back to Coffee and Bailey and the safety of Tzu Kingdom.

"MY TEDDY MY TEDDY!" screamed the baby suddenly. "SHE IS MY ONLY FRIEND..... IN THE BACK OF THE KENNEL. PLEASE, I CAN'T GO ANYWHERE WITHOUT MILLICENT" and started to cry, quite uncontrollably and extraordinarily loudly this time.

"It's only a teddy bear, we can get another one." said Phoebe, who had a job to do that didn't include rescuing teddy bears, and, to be honest, she wasn't really one for cuddling toys anyway.

"But, but I love her.....MILLICENT....." she started to wriggle out of Paddy's arms in an effort to get back to the kennel.

'She's not only a teddy bear,' thought Stanley, 'she's all she has in the world and if she goes back for her we might lose her to that nasty woman'.

"I'll get her for you." He said and, with all his courage, he ran back to the dirty, ramshackle kennel and retrieved the muddy, smelly, pink and white teddy bear and picked it up in his teeth. But, he certainly hadn't realised the amount of barking that had come out of the baby tzu when she realised she had left Millicent behind.

As he came out of the kennel, the great lofty, imposing, nasty lady was blocking his way.

She had seen Paddy and Phoebe running away with her money-making puppy machine and she was dreadfully angry. What's more, Stanley was looking a long way up, face to face with her, and he was terrified.

Then he remembered something Mama had said earlier in the week when they were playing in the snow as the lady stomped towards him... "Stop running around my legs Stanners...you will trip me up". I'm going to stop her, he thought, and I know how.

As brave as a lion, for he was tzu, he ran around and around her. There was a lot further to go around the nasty lady than there was around Mama's slender ankles. He ran faster and faster until the lady had quite lost her balance...she stumbled, fell on her face in the mud and he was free! He picked up Millicent the teddy bear and ran, as fast as his legs would carry him.

"WWWWWUUUUUUBBBNNNNN" he shouted to the others, his voice muffled by Millicent, and run they did, right through the doors, down the fairy corridors and right back to the kingdom with a newly recruited baby tzu safe in their arms.

And Millicent the teddy bear bobbing happily in Stanley's mouth.

Chapter 9

THE rescue team arrived back at Tzu Kingdom to a huge cheer from the tzus who had stayed to witness their return, as well as many tzus who had arrived from other parts of the world and joined the anxious wait for the completion of the rescue mission.

King Bailey and Queen Coffee were visibly relieved to see their return, especially little Stanley. Coffee took the wide-eyed baby tzu from Paddy's arms so Bailey could give him a welcome back hug.

The little rescued tzu was now nervously chewing Millicent the teddy's ear and, with wide frightened eyes, was trying to take in everything that was going on around her. She had never seen so many Tzus and, well, Tzu Kingdom was something to behold on any normal day - for someone who had just been through a rescue, it was almost too much. She started to cry and whimper. Coffee cuddled her in close and kissed her on her nose and each ear, in the way she had done to Stanley when she first met him

"I'm going to take her straight down to the Comforter Wing, Mabel and Myrtle are here tonight from New Zealand so she will be as well looked after as she possibly could be."

The Queen rushed off, holding the distraught, grubby, crying baby tight and talking softly and gently to her as she ran.

Stanley had a funny feeling in his tummy; it was as if butterflies were fluttering about in it. He had felt it for the first time when he spoke to her in the kennel and he guessed it was either all the excitement of rescuing the teddy bear or too much gravy.

"It's Stanley you should be hugging KB....I think we have found one of the bravest tzus EVER!"

Paddy explained how the newest recruit had risked his life to run back and get the teddy bear and delighted the King and the gathered masses with the dramatic re-enacted story of how he had made the nasty lady fall over!

Of course, there was a very serious side to this and the senior tzus listened with horror as they heard about the puppy farming that was in store for the baby tzu.

King Bailey looked at the clock and gasped.

"It's late Stanley and, young man, it's time you went home to your mama and dad. You might be brave, but I have to insist, little dogs need their sleep!"

He came close and hugged him.

"We are all very proud of you young Stanley – what an adventure on your first visit to Tzu Kingdom. The comforters will look after the little tzu, why don't you pop back tomorrow and see how she is getting on? And, we need a little chat about safety and obedience I think!"

Stanley smiled, both sheepishly and sleepily.

"Colin" said the King, "could you escort this young fellow home and make sure he knows how to open and close the fairy doors safely."

A quiet tzu wearing an artist's smock hopped down from a bar stool where he had been drawing on a sketch pad and tucked his work under his front paw, clasping it tightly. He limped over to them, slowly yet confidently.

Oh, thought Stanley. "Colin" Colin.

Chapter 10

COLIN Shih Tzu smiled at Stanley, wiped his pencil-covered artist's paw on his smock and extended it in the warmest and friendliest of greetings.

"Hi" he said putting his other paw over the whole pawshake "I'm Colin, it's lovely to meet you. I love meeting new pals....well it's my job! So, I suppose I had better get you home...King's orders! Follow me, I go a bit slow so just go at your own pace and we will get to know each other."

He was one of the nicest, warmest tzus he had met so far, and he was up against some stiff competition!

Stanley slowed down to keep time with Colin, if truth be told he did have quite a limp in his back leg and he wondered if it would be impolite to ask what happened when he offered up the information himself.

"I suppose you are wondering about my limp then?"

"Erm, just a little bit, I didn't know if I was allowed to ask about it and I wouldn't want to upset you."

"Oh it's fine, it's no secret! It was sustained in the line of duty, when I was training to be a rescuer a few dog years back; I wasn't much older than you are now..."

Chapter 11

COLIN was full of energy when he was a puppy. He was the first to volunteer for anything and he had his heart set on being a rescuer from when he first saw Tanner bring back a Tzu called Quincy from a filthy scrapyard where he had been tied up with a piece of string all day and night. He wasn't a young tzu and he had spent most of his life being treated this way. Quincy landed on his paws when he got a home with a lovely retired lady with wild blonde hair and lived out the winter of his life in luxury, turning up at the Tzu Kingdom parties with snacks for everyone, keen to show his gratitude at being rescued. Tanner was an inspiration to young Colin for rescuing Quincy.

So when he turned two in human years (fourteen dog years) he sat his rescuer exams with the Tzus of Experience and passed with flying colours. He got an A+ in all three papers and 100% in his practical exam. He wanted to do nothing else.

He trained with Tanner and, by the time another dog year had passed, he was a fully qualified rescuer.

Colin was also the first to qualify under new King Bailey and he puffed with pride when he was presented with his Rescuer Badge....to be worn at all time on duty.

He was so proud of himself, but on his first mission after he qualified, it all went horribly wrong.

The scouts had heard of a small dog called Paddy, now a scout himself, just four months old and living in a garage with no love at all. King Bailey, ruling alone before he made Coffee his queen and still ever so sad at the recent passing of his best friend King Pierre, agreed that they should mount an urgent rescue. Young Colin volunteered and was accepted as the fifth member of an extensive rescue operation.

They went through the fairy doors and agreed that Rescuers Lennon and Tanner would go in to the garage through a broken door to grab the boy.

It all went well. The little tzu was more than happy to leave his stinky home and took Tanner's paw to run back to Tzu Kingdom. He was excited about the fairy doors and he couldn't wait to be magically shrunk to size!

Just as they got through the garage door, Paddy's captor came back and Colin simply couldn't help himself. He felt his ears going red, his tail going stiff and he told the man exactly what he thought of him.

That's when it happened. The man kicked him. He hurt him and he cried in pain.

Lennon scooped up Paddy and the injured, screaming Colin and ran as fast as he could towards the fairy doors. They all leapt through them and escaped.

Colin's injuries were worse than they feared, the comforter tzus came running as soon as they heard, with King Bailey in hot pursuit.

Bailey knew that this was something that only Human Tzu Parents could deal with and four of the strongest tzus carried Colin carefully through the fairy corridors to his home.

When they got there, they took Colin as close to the house as they dared and barked and howled. As soon as they saw his parents, Dadsy and Pops, come running to the back door they retreated to the bottom of the garden. They watched as they picked him up, both wondering what could have possibly happened as one of them took a phone out of his pocket and rang the vet whilst the other cradled Colin in to his jumper.

Colin was crying but, knowing their job was done, the tzus returned to Tzu Kingdom so as not to give away its secrets.

The King was inconsolable; he never wanted anyone to get hurt on his watch. Although he knew Colin had taken an unnecessary risk, he blamed himself for sending a newly qualified tzu on such a dangerous mission.

'I'm just not sure I am worthy of being King' thought Bailey to himself. He had been an excellent deputy to King Pierre as he got older and unsteady, yet doing it on his own? Well, that was another matter entirely.

As tears started to fall down his furry face, he felt a soft paw on his. It was Coffee.

"Sweetie, you don't have to do this on your own you know."

She hugged him, absorbing his tears into her soft, silky fur.

Chapter 12

"WHAT happened next?" said Stanley, reflecting on how similar his first mission had been and how close he had come to ending up in the V.E.T. like Colin did. It actually scared him more than he would like to admit and, as much as he loved Tzu Kingdom, he couldn't wait to see Mama and Daddy, now that they had been talking about Colin cuddling his dads.

"Well, I needed an operation on my leg to make it work again and I had to wear bandages for ages. It was a long time before I was able to come back through the fairy doors because I couldn't risk the shrinking. Sometimes, the gang would come through and check I was OK.

"I missed quite a lot. Whilst I was away, Bailey and Coffee got married and announced that they would serve equally together as King and Queen of Tzus. I was so happy for them, they eloped to Paris to get married and only had three guests — Old King Pierre's young brother and sister Franc and Centime and, of course, Coffee's best friend Nancy was her bridesmaid. I kept sending messages back to tell Bailey it was my own silly fault, well, me and my big gob, but he wouldn't hear of it."

"I presume it was only the fact that he had his Coffee by his side that convinced him to stay as King, even though all the tzus adore him!"

Then, Colin shook himself and announced that it actually was that time that little tzus went back home to their families and that he wouldn't be leaving it too late himself to get back to Notting Hill for bed.

"We will talk more another day young Stanley. Don't worry about the little one, we will take care of her and you can visit her soon.

"And Stanley....you really are as brave as a lion."

Chapter 13

WITH a whopping swoosh noise, Stanley finally landed back in his garden, in the shadow of Edinburgh Castle. He noticed how it tickled when you went through the fairy doors and how, soon afterwards, he always did a loud burp like Paddy had warned! He giggled, and then heard Mama shouting his name as she ran down the steps with her worried face on.

"Oh Stanners, there you are my baby, where have you been all this time! You've been out here more than ten minutes — what is the fascination with this old tree?"

She picked him up and cuddled him, kissing the top of his head. He was so pleased to see her that he kissed her back excitedly and even though he loved Tzu Kingdom and all his friends, he was especially pleased to see Mama. He felt safest of all in her arms and that was never going to change. Not ever.

As they went indoors Stanley saw the time — 6.15pm — and nearly time for Daddy to return home. He jumped down from Mama's arms because he had another important "dog of the house" job to do... await his return at the front door and alert the street when his big blue car came in to view.

He knew it was Friday night so there would be something delicious for dinner and, although he had eaten plenty of snacks at King Bailey's party, he figured he would be able to find room for whatever was on offer.

41

After half an hour's wait, Daddy was home and Stan barked excitedly at his return so everyone in hearing distance knew that he was home and was safe. He wanted to tell them both all about his day, the rescue, the dancing, Colin, Coffee, Paddy, Phoebe, the baby tzu rescue....and that's when he remembered. Tzu Kingdom had to be a secret like the fairies had been promised all those hundreds of dog years ago.

So, instead, after helping his human parents eat a Chinese takeaway he fell asleep by the fire, dreaming sweet dreams about all the exciting and adventurous things that had happened. He dreamt about going back tomorrow and seeing all his new Tzu pals, as well as checking on a certain pretty little tzu with a pink teddy!

"Is he roaring in his sleep down there?" said Daddy.

"I think he jolly well is, bless our little lion dog!" said Mama.

Chapter 14

SATURDAY morning arrived and, most unusually, Mama and Daddy were up early making toast and strong coffee.

"We've got an exciting day today my boy..." said Daddy.

'I know,' thought Stanley, 'I'm going to Tzu Kingdom after breakfast to see the pretty tzu I rescued and I am going to take her some flowers from our pretty garden to make her feel happy and better.' This once again, he noticed, made him feel all fluttery and upside down in his tummy.

"...we are going to meet Granny and have a big day out with all the family and we are staying at her house tonight."

'Well, this is going to scupper my plans,' thought the little vanilla tzu, wondering if there was a way to Tzu Kingdom at Granny's. On the contrary, from there he wasn't sure where all the fairy doors would be and what if he couldn't find his way back. He remembered how Tanner had to take a break from being a rescuer whilst he was on holiday with his family.

"Are you alright baby? You're usually so excited about going to Granny's...we are going out for yummy food in the café by the castle...." said Mama.

What a dilemma this gave him — Granny was one of his favourite people. He loved eating out with his family and he got to stay over at Granny's cosy cottage where he had his own bed by Mama and Daddy's and yet, he desperately wanted to go back to Tzu Kingdom today and check on the little one.

'I'm leading a double life here' he thought, and wished he could be in two places at once.

An hour later, with his seat belt engaged for safety in the back of the car and his overnight bag packed, they all headed off for Granny's. As he dozed in the back, he overheard a conversation and quickly picked up the gist of it and he felt terrible, and more than a bit worried.

"Look, he's so quiet I don't think he's awfully well. If he's not perked up after lunch then I suppose we had better head back home and take him to the vets...."

'Oh my,' thought Stanley, 'that is the LAST thing I want to happen'. He knew he had pushed things too far and now he was worrying Mama and Daddy.

Stan had a stern conversation with himself in his head. He knew he had to get things in perspective. He had a lovely life in Edinburgh where he was the dog of the house and he also had a magical place he could go to and be an important tzu and dance the Paw Stomp. He knew he would go to Tzu Kingdom very soon however, he couldn't upset Mama, Daddy and Granny — that would be a naughty thing to do. He had to fix this.

He sat bolt upright in the back of the car, woofed his apologies to his parents and made it quite clear that he was very much looking forward to a family day after all.

Mama and Daddy laughed as Stan proceeded to show them just how very well he was by wagging his tail, barking at the cars that went past and singing along to the radio.

"Oh Stanners, no vet visit for you my boy....you are the funny one!" laughed Mama as they all cheerfully sang along to the radio as the hurtled along the road.

'Sunday morning, as soon as we are back, it's Tzu Kingdom here I come!'

Chapter 15

SWOOOOSH. Tickle! Burp! Double burp! Stanley was back in Tzu Kingdom at long last!

He had a magnificent time with his family and there had been much laughter and food — some of his favourite things! He had seen his uncles and aunts and cousins, as well as Granny, and they had all played with him lots. He did quite well on the posh food front too — everyone wanted to give him a bit of their dinner, especially the younger humans, so he had a tummy full of burgers, sausages and chips by the time they had got home.

It had been a late night and they had been singing along to Mama's favourite songs back at Granny's. He must have been singing awfully loud, because Mama and Daddy both had headaches this morning. Granny didn't look too chirpy either but she cooked them bacon and egg sandwiches just the same, as always. He had a lovely cuddle with Granny...she was wonderful! She was a brilliant cook and an excellent cuddler too! He was so happy because he knew he was lucky to have her and she had also knitted him two wonderful woolly blankets — one at home and one here, in front of the fire. It made him reflect on the little one-less-fortunate and wondered if she would soon be living somewhere where she would have a blanket and a family of her own.

They got home just before lunchtime and Mama announced she had to catch up with business things on the computer so, Stanley asked to go out to the garden. He knew he would only be a few minutes in "home" time so he could run down to the big tree and get through to his Tzu Kingdom pals and be back to help her like he normally did – sitting beside her as her official "Office Assistant". Daddy was catching up on his snoozes in front of the television watching football so he knew he could finally pop to his other life.

At the tree, he barked loud and firm like Paddy and Colin had showed him. As before, the fairies opened the doors, he felt himself shrink down and he was straight through arriving safely on the other side.

Once he had pardoned himself for burping, in case anyone had heard him, he looked around. It was the first time he had been through on his own and, before, he'd only followed one of the other tzus through to the Party Room except this time, he had time to take in what he saw.

It was beautiful. He was in the Welcome Room or the "Meet and Greet" as some called it. He couldn't imagine anywhere more welcoming. It was a round room, with music playing and it had plush sofas and beanbags all around as well as water and food bowls with signs asking you to help yourself, take a seat and wait for a Welcomer.

It was then that he realised where the music was coming from – in the corner with their guitars were Colin and an older tzu with a long, crazy beard and curly tzu ears wearing a denim jacket, little round sunglasses and beads. He ran over excitedly, wagging his tail at them both.

"Hello, young man!" said the older tzu.

"Stanley!" shouted Colin, swinging round and so pleased to see his familiar and enthusiastic little face. "Lennon, this is Stanley..." they shook paws warmly, tails wagging even faster. "Lennon is one of my colleagues here in the Welcome Room – he plays guitar in the kingdom band "Tzu Aroo" and he's been teaching me. It's fab, come to a lesson one day or one of the gigs in the Party Room. We usually play on Tuesdays and you can sing along with everyone... we put the words up on the chalkboard."

Stan made a diary note in his head.

"I've heard so much about you Stanley; you've made quite an impression on everyone after your heroics on Friday night. I must say, the little girl tzus can't talk of anything else when they come through!" said Lennon.

Stanley blushed. Well, this was a bit embarrassing.... girls!

"Our little artist here, Colin, drew a picture of you and they are all swooning over it...you're like a rock star!" He laughed.

Stanley got even more embarrassed and shook his long ears in front of his face so he could hide from the conversation!

"Don't get embarrassed Stan..." said Colin "it's probably my drawings they're swooning at!"

Colin and Lennon laughed. Stanley smiled coyly; quite aware that the fellows were taking the mickey!

"Anyway" said Colin, giving him a hug, "we are pleased to see you; someone has been waiting for you..."

"The baby tzu?" said Stanley, with a sparkle in his eyes, his tail up in the air and a flutter in his tummy once again.

"Oh, erm, maybe, I suppose so...but first King Bailey and Phoebe the Rescuer need a word about the rescue mission you went on." said Colin.

Stan pulled his serious face. He had a horrible feeling that he was in an enormous amount of trouble.

Chapter 16

LENNON asked the worried Stanley to follow him to the Royal Room where the King and Queen had their thrones and office.

'Oh no, this is it,' thought the little tzu, 'I am going to get banned for being naughty and disobedient,' as he reluctantly followed elder Lennon down a corridor, his tail dragging on the floor behind him.

Lennon pushed the towering wooden doors open to reveal two high thrones covered in velvet on top of some steps. Stanley assumed, rightly, that these were the ceremonial thrones of Tzu Kingdom and that Bailey and Coffee should be sitting on them, although there was no-one there. He looked about and there were Bailey, Coffee and Phoebe sitting curled up on colourful bean bags, chatting earnestly. They all looked up and smiled but, even though they didn't look that cross, Stanley started to get very upset and he was whimpering although trying not to show it. Of course, there was no way that his upset face was going to get past their lovely Queen.

"What's the matter?" she said, running over and kissing the top of his head whilst stroking his ears.

"I'm sorry, I really am, please don't banish me from Tzu Kingdom....please....I will be good...I'm sorry I was so naughty...I promise to behave in future...." his nose started to run and he was in a terrible kerfuffle.

"Oh, little Stanley, we would never do that!" she cuddled him until he calmed down and stopped shaking.

"No never! Don't worry about that little chap, that's not what we do here!" said King Bailey, laughing in his kind, friendly way. "But we must ensure the safety of our rescue teams, well, all in Tzu Kingdom, or Coffee and I would not be doing our jobs! We just need to discuss what happens and any untoward incidents, that's why Phoebe is here, as she was leading this rescue."

Coffee passed Stanley a tissue from her cardigan pocket and he wiped his tears away and blew his nose, holding out the hanky once he'd finished, because he didn't know what else to do with it. Coffee took it over to the bin. Recovered from his upset, he sat up neatly for the rescue mission de-brief as Phoebe perused her notes.

Phoebe stood up from her beanbag, smoothed over her fur, cleared her throat with a little cough and read aloud:

"Friday night's rescue of the baby tzu: Incident report by Phoebe, Senior Rescuer."

"The team comprised of Alice, Paddy, Pom Pom, Stanley and me."

"The Coax and Sweep rescue began as planned with Paddy and Stanley on "coax" duty and Alice and Pom Pom on "sweep" duty with me as mission lead. Following the rescue of the baby tzu from the dirty kennel she became distressed when we were running back to the kennel when she realised that she had not picked up her teddy — known as "Millicent" - when we left. There was some considerable concern that she would wriggle out of Paddy's arms and run away, putting herself and the five tzu rescue team at risk from the nasty lady.

"Stanley Vanilla Tzu, who was just standing in for Tanner on his first night in Tzu Kingdom, put himself, and indeed all six of us, at risk when he made a snap decision to return to the kennel to retrieve the teddy bear."

Stanley looked at the floor and shuffled his paws.

Oops.

"Unfortunately, the nasty lady had heard us and was waiting outside the kennel for Stanley when he came out with the teddy bear. However, in an act of extreme cleverness, he tripped the lady up, grabbed the item in his teeth and shouted to all of us to run and we did, right back to safety.

"Therefore, there were no injuries sustained in the rescue mission and it was completed fully, with a rescued baby tzu safe in our world."

Gosh, she's very business-like and quite impressive, thought Stanley.

"There are two main lessons to be learnt from this experience. One, ensure that the rescue site is thoroughly scanned for any precious belongings (even teddy bears) or other tzu and two, that tzus must always work in pairs, staying with their partner as indicated by the mission leader, and not go all gung-ho."

She looked straight at Stanley, as did Coffee and Bailey.

Double oops. Stanley felt ever so ashamed, like the time Mama told him off for helping himself to a man's curry in the park near home. Even though it was very tasty, and the man had eaten all he wanted to, he knew that wasn't the right thing to do although, he mused, at least he didn't have to endure this dressing down with a bright yellow curry-stained tzu beard and a burning hot tongue.

"However, having discussed the rescue with Paddy, Alice and Pom Pom we are all agreed that he made the right decision under difficult circumstances and, therefore, I would like to recommend, my dear friends King Bailey and Queen Coffee, that Stanley be offered a place on Rescuer Training School so we can make the most of his quick thinking and lion-like courage."

Stanley almost fell over with pride!

"Is this something you want to do Stanley?" asked King Bailey.

He didn't know what to say to the King. He was so proud of himself, he was still new to Tzu Kingdom and he already knew there were lots of opportunities here for him.

Coffee stroked his ears again.

"Sweetheart, you don't have to decide right now, it's not even a week since we met! It's a real honour and Phoebe and Tanner would be proud to train you, but it's an important decision and they'll understand if you want to take some time to think it through. There's other things you can do too, like being a scout like Paddy or a comforter, or you can just enjoy the parties and make friends. Think about it, there's no rush but what a compliment for you!"

"I will Queen Coffee, thank you...erm, there is something I do want to do very much though. Please can I see the baby tzu we rescued?"

"Of course, come on, de-brief over. Let's go to the Comforter Wing and see how she's doing."

Stanley skipped off after his Queen, with his tummy butterflies doing somersaults.

Chapter 17

"MABEL, Myrtle" Queen Coffee hollered as she pushed open the door to the Comforter Wing. "Where are you?" Stanley followed her in slowly, his eyes like saucers as he took in another beautiful place in the Kingdom. Of course, it was filled with beanbags again.

"We're here Little Miss Coffee Cup Sugar Lump! Yoo hoo...in the kitchen, we're just making some more soup and a few sandwiches for patient lunches. Come on in....." came the response.

She laughed and turned to him to explain.

"They've known me since I was a puppy Stanley, long before I was Queen. They are like mothers to me, they are so lovely. They are New Zealanders, they love things traditional so everything here is cooked from scratch, the beds are soft and fragrant and, well, they have little pet names for everyone I do believe! You will have one yourself by the end of your visit I don't doubt! They're sisters too — I adore them both — they're a little bit embarrassing for us all sometimes — most of us have been to them with a little hurty or an upset tummy and, well, it's almost impossible for them not to look after you... even if you are King and Queen."

"They love caring for our rescued tzus and they'll never retire, although I wish they could. I don't know if you know but, well, King Bailey was rescued when he was a young dog from a terrible situation and they nursed him back to health over many, many weeks until he was better. Stanley....well, if he hadn't been rescued....ten minutes later and.....we may never have had our lovely King Bailey." Her eyes went all teary and, for the first time, Stanley put his paw out to comfort her, instead of the other way round.

'She loves our King Bailey deeply,' he thought.

She wiped her tears, shook her fur all over and smiled. "Come through to the kitchen and meet them....I hope you like soup!"

Chapter 18

MABEL and Myrtle were just adorable! They were both grey and white long haired tzus and, in a way, they reminded him of Granny, if she was a tzu which, of course, she wasn't.

They were singing happily together and doing a little dance as they boiled up soup for the poorly tzus in their care. There was very little to tell them apart, so he addressed them both when he spoke to them.

On a chalkboard in the kitchen there was a list of current patients and Stanley saw that there were five rescues in at the moment. The list read:

Boys' Room: Percy; Sammy; Brickie & Hiro

Girls' Room: Maisie

"Is Maisie who I think it is?" he asked them.

"Well, that depends on whether you think it is the pretty little baby tzu you rescued little Mr Stanley Pops Pudding Pie" said one of them (he still wasn't sure which one) as he blushed and smiled. "She can't wait to see you cutie, she's talked about nothing else other than how you rescued Millicent for her! It's all 'My Stanley is so brave. My Stanley is so handsome. My Stanley runs so fast...'"

He was so excited – it had been days since the rescue and he wondered if she would even remember him. From what Mabel & Myrtle said, it looked like she did and he was so relieved!

Coffee spoke to them both, excitedly,

"Oh, ladies, you've named her after your little sister – that's beautiful. Stanley, when the girls were young they had another sister, she was an unwell girl and, well, she was gone too soon, less than a year old. She was called Maisie you see, such a sweet little thing."

"Well, the littl'un looked so much like her and she has such a fiery spirit and adorable sense of humour that we just knew, at last, this was the one that deserved to share little Maisie's name. Plus, she does love her teddy bear, just like our little sis did." said Mable or Myrtle.

"So, young man, I suppose you'd like to go see her? Come here, let's tidy you up...."

Before he could protest, the ladies were at him with brushes and combs, smoothing down his fur, straightening up his bow tie and fluffing his tail. Honestly, they really were like Granny.

"She's in the girls' room Stanley, she's the only little girl we have in at the moment so she will be glad of the company. She's looking a lot better than when you last saw her, she's been up and about today; I am sure that she's finally caught up on some rest now she's all cosy and clean and she would love some company."

Mabel (or Myrtle) opened the door to a very pink room and there, in a spacious pink four poster bed covered with a flowery duvet and cuddling the little pink and white teddy bear that he had retrieved only two days earlier was the most beautiful Shih Tzu Stanley had ever seen....

Maisie.

Chapter 19

"STANLEY!!!!!!" screamed Maisie as she jumped out of the squishiness. With Millicent still in her paws she kissed Stanley all over and hugged him, whilst jumping up and down and wagging her tail.

"You rescued me AND Millicent...I love you so much my handsome, brave rescuer. I have missed you so much! Where have you been?"

More kisses were planted all over his fur and he jumped around and around with her with his tummy butterflies jumping on the inside too!

"I have been trying to get back but Mama and Daddy had plans and I had to do important things with my Granny and I have been trying and....I MISSED YOU TOO!!! I LOVE YOU MAISIE!"

Gosh, I love her, thought Stanley! This finally explained the fluttery tummy butterflies...he was in love with Maisie! It all made sense now.

"Look my Stanley....look at my tidy pretty claws, look at my sparkly clean teeth, smell my shampooed fur... feel how soft it is ...and just LOOK at Millicent!" she said as she shoved her now clean, soapy smelling teddy at Stanley's nose. Maisie, herself, looked scrummy in a pair of pink pyjamas and a fluffy dressing gown that swept across the floor when she walked, as if she was a princess.

Myrtle entered the room, pushing a little trolley with two steaming hot soups in large bowls with handles, six slices of toast, a plate of jammy biscuits and a large bowl of water.

"Stanley Cutey Pie, don't get young Maisie Moo Moppet Top over-excited, she's not quite better yet and we don't want any setbacks. Why don't you both come over here and have some lunch!"

Holding paws, they went over and cuddled up on a bean bag together, holding the bowl handles and slurping the soup, laughing when it dribbled down their tzu beards. They shared the buttery toast with Millicent and, over the jammy biscuits, Maisie began to tell her Stanley just what had happened since they last saw each other...

Chapter 20

QUEEN Coffee hugged me all the way down the long, windy corridors and straight in to the Comforter Wing. I cried all the way, I mean, you all seemed lovely and everything except I was very scared, with all these kings and queens and so many tzus looking at me, and I still couldn't believe you had rescued Millicent for me or that Paddy had grabbed me or that we went through that little door in the tree!

Everything in Tzu Kingdom is pretty and smells divine and Coffee, well, she smells all of Maple Syrup and raspberry shampoo. She's said I am to think of her as my temporary mummy until she can find me a charming home where I am going to be loved forever. She said this is called a "Foster Mum" I call her Fosty Coffee and, you know, I reckon I always will!

All my fur was yucky, dirty and stuck together and I didn't smell very pleasant did I? Well, as soon as I got here Mabel and Myrtle gave me a glass of milk and then some banana bread to build up my strength. It was delicious and it made me stop crying too.

While I was eating my banana bread, Coffee ran me a warm, soapy bubbly bath in a little round tub but, before I could get in, Mabel and Myrtle had to cut my fur all short. They said it will grow back in no time but it was too spoilt and it was hurting my skin and making me sore. I cried again, then Coffee cuddled me and said that it would all grow back soon but they would at least keep my tail fur long like a tzu tail should be and that she would personally detangle it with her very own Royal nimble tzu paws. And she did. Look! Isn't she the best?

I had never had a bath before so I was a bit scared, but I absolutely loved it. The water was warm and it soothed my hurty skin, and as I soaked my paws in the water I started to feel so much better. Coffee massaged me all over and then picked me up in a warm, fluffy towel and dried me by the fireplace whilst I ate some soup. I had never felt so special and they said just to ask if I want anything to eat or drink.

Then, after me, it was Millicent's turn! Mabel put her in the bath and scrub-a-dub-dubbed her all over and then pegged her out over the bath to drip dry. She's not dirty anymore; she's the cleanest, nicest smelling teddy bear in the whole world! Look how pink her pink is!

When we were both dry and supper had gone down into our tummies, Fosty Coffee brought us through here and gave me some pink pyjamas to wear. I'd never had things of my own before and I couldn't believe how lucky I was. I slept, cuddling Millicent, like I had never slept before. There were no scary noises, I wasn't cold and it wasn't dark or smelly, because the Comforters had put twinkly lights at the bottom of the bed and all the sheets and pillows smelt of marmalade. All I could hear was Mabel and Myrtle chatting quietly in the kitchen before they went home to New Zealand to see their family. In the morning, when I woke up, there were two new tzus – Franc and Centime from Paris – here looking after me and the boys next door and they made us bacon and scrambly eggs for breakfast.

After breakfast, we all went out to play in the little fairy garden outside to get fresh air to make us better. The boys were funny – we played ball and I think they let me win every time. They are all brothers you know – Percy, Sammy, Hiro and Brickie – they got rescued the week before me because they were abandoned. It sounds terrifying – they were left in a box by the side of a road before the scouts found them and the King sent a rescue team to bring them to Tzu Kingdom.

I started to feel a little bit better so Franc and Centime made us a picnic in the garden....enormous platefuls of sandwiches! For afters we had coconut ice cream and honey biscuits.

Then we went snoozing on the beanbags all together. When we woke up it was evening time and Mabel and Myrtle were back and making soup for dinner! I can barely keep up with all the eating! The boys are stronger already so they had some soup and toast. I was so tired and full that I got put to bed with milk and biscuits.

I had another beautiful night of sleep and then I woke up, I had some eggy soldiers for breakfast and then you were here...my hero!

Maisie and Stanley cuddled up on the beanbag and carried on chatting away until Mabel or Myrtle came in with some sandwiches and water.

"What are you two talking about for so long?" she said.

"Oh, just 'tzu stuff' I guess" said Stanley, to Maisie's giggles.

And they were too. And they carried on talking about tzu stuff every day after that.

They sat frontways on the bean bag and waved their tails to compare how fluffy they were.

They laid backways and waved their paws in the air, comparing the cuteness of their paws.

They stood sideways and measured their ears and beards against each other.

They stood standways and measured how tall they were against the wall.

They stood noseways and looked at their reflection in the water bowl and compared their little noses and whiskers.

Myrtle looked on, with a tear in her eye yet a happy smile on her face.

"Are you thinking what I'm thinking?" said Mabel as she finished serving up food to their patients.

"I think so sister! Do they remind you of Coffee and Bailey too?"

"It's like history repeating itself and it is adorable. Except it was Bailey who arrived in the terrible state and Coffee who nursed him back to health and made him the super King he is today."

"I just have a hunch that these two have a very big future ahead of them here in Tzu Kingdom."

Chapter 21

MAISIE was getting stronger every time Stanley visited and also getting better and better at playing football with the four tzu brothers next door. She might have been small, yet she was feisty and had scored more goals than all the boys put together.

He did rather suspect that they were all jolly decent enough to let her win most of the time because none of them wanted to see her upset after the terrible time she had had.

But then, one day, the boys were sad and didn't want to play football at all.

"We are to leave in the morning," explained Brickie, looking despondent.

"Leave?" said Maisie and Stanley together, with shock in their voices.

"Where are you going?" said Stanley.

"To new homes. With people," said Sammy. "We would rather stay here amongst our own kind where we are happy. We all love Tzu Kingdom but King Bailey says we are better and we have to go."

"I suppose it wasn't to last after all...." Hiro sighed, looking at his brothers with sadness.

Stanley wasn't sure about this. Why would King Bailey banish the boys from Tzu Kingdom when he said he wouldn't do such a thing? He needed to know so, on his way home from lunch with Maisie he decided he had to be brave as a lion once again and do something about it.

He was going to see the King of Tzus and ask him to explain exactly what was going on. He would stomp his paw if necessary, even if it was to the King.

He walked and walked down the corridor to the Royal Chamber, trying not to be nervous or scared. "I'm as brave as a lion, as brave as a lion, as brave as a lion..." he repeated under his breath time and time again.

When he arrived at the door that Lennon had taken him to a few weeks earlier he had never felt less like a lion. He was still a little bit scared of the King – what if he wasn't so warm-hearted after all? What if he had been wrong or fibbed to? Maybe he did banish tzus. He was scared, not of asking Bailey an important question, but of learning something he didn't want to know.

He knocked on the door softly and no one heard him. He leaned on the door so it opened just a little bit... "Hello....?" and heard some voices. He listened; they were quietly discussing something that he found quite disturbing.

"Should we split them in to two pairs or leave them all together?" It was Queen Coffee.

"It depends on where we put them really my love," said the second voice...it was King Bailey.

'Oh my dog....they ARE going to be banished,' he realised in horror.

"I sense we are best off leaving them in Manchester together..." said a third voice and he couldn't believe it.....that was Paddy's voice.

The shock of hearing that his trusted pal Paddy was part of the conspiracy made him stumble and, all of a sudden, he fell against the door and crashed in to the Royal Chamber in a heap!

"STANLEY!" they all gasped.

"How could you banish the boys?" he said, in an angry voice. I thought you were all wonderful tzus and I have made friends with them and now you are going to banish them and you said you wouldn't. You're going to banish Maisie next I just know it…" he stomped all his paws.

Bailey, Coffee and Paddy all laughed and made him even more cross. He stomped his paws again, even harder this time.

"Stanley, don't be silly! Come and sit down and stop paw stomping. We are taking the boys to safety, we're not banishing any tzu!" said the King.

He didn't know whether to run away or sit down as he'd been asked, but he knew he had to protect Maisie so, although unsure, he went and sat down next to them, with his crossest face on, crossed his legs and listened to Bailey's explanation.

"Young fella, I think you worry too much. It is a lovely trait to care so deeply, although I don't suppose the boys quite listened properly given how busy they are eating toast and playing football! If you unsure, you must ask and without making a big fuss!"

"Tzus don't live in Tzu Kingdom — we all have our own families just like you have your Mama and Daddy… I have a human mum in England and Coffee has a Momma and Dad in Canada….we go home to them of course, enjoying the best of both worlds". Stanley hadn't even thought about where they all lived and whether they had families — he had just assumed that they slept in the Royal Chamber and were always here waiting for him on their beanbags. Then he remembered what Maisie had said about Mabel and Myrtle going home to their families, he knew about Old King Pierre living in Paris and it all made a bit more sense.

"When we rescue tzus from bad situations we get them well again — well enough to find a family of their own and we make sure that we put them in a place where they will find their forever family. Occasionally, if we don't feel that we can make them better with soup and love then we make a decision to put them with a Knower. That's how we do good, like our forefurs promised the fairies all those years ago.

Paddy added his own wisdom to the explanation.

"We Scouts does lots of different stuff — we find those who need rescuing, we look out for tzus to invite them in 'ere, we find the right homes for the needy and, well, we keep an eye on all what's going on and everything...right up until we say goodbye even."

"What do you mean by "say goodbye" Paddy?" he asked, with his innocent eyes looking hopefully at his friend.

"Well" said Paddy, "we all has our time on the earth and, well, there's a time when we are all old and, well, we....we....."

"We all die one day Stanley," said the King.

Stanley gulped. "When?" he said, with his eyes as wide as dinner plates, blinking nervously.

"Mostly when we are old, when our little bodies just can't cope anymore and we have to say goodbye. Like Pierre, King before me. I miss Pierre. He was fifteen in human years when he went to sleep for the last time."

The room fell silent as Stanley took this sad information in and Coffee and Bailey thought of their dear friend Pierre in his younger days. Such a funny and organised king, he'd been the one who had started the Friday night parties and no-one would ever forget him!

Paddy broke the silence; wasn't comfortable thinking about anyone falling asleep for the last time. He had an older brother, Mitch, at home who had long since stopped coming to Tzu Kingdom mainly because it gave him terrible wind and he preferred to stay at home with their human family. He liked his sleep and snuggles on the sofa nowadays, although he did still love hearing about all Paddy's adventures and said he might pop through for a Christmas party. Once Mitch started burping, he found it difficult to stop!

"So about these pupsters then...."

"Oh yes...we aren't banishing the boys sweetie." said Queen Coffee "we are going to make sure they have some forever homes...all of them."

Stanley knew this made sense; of course no fur was being banished. In truth he felt a little bit silly. He still had so much to learn about the workings of Tzu Kingdom.

"We were just wondering if they were more likely to get adopted together if we put them in to the human world in two sets of two or all together — four puppies might get split up, you see, into singles but a pair might find a home together."

"I feel they would do well at Manchester Dogs Home" said Paddy. "There's a lovely Knower there called Debs and she is a real tzu lover. I reckon she will make sure they go two by two. I think we put them in a safety box, alert Debs and get them in to the rehoming centre. They'll find homes in no time at all being so cute!"

"What's a Knower?" asked Stanley.

"It's a Human-that-knows - someone we trust and knows some of what Tzu Kingdom is all about. We sort of 'put tzus in their paths' so we know they are taken care of! It worked for Bailey..."

King Bailey nodded in agreement.

"Will they ever come back to Tzu Kingdom?" he asked.

"Of course, sweetie" said Coffee....the scouts keep an eye on all the tzus we know as best they can and when the time is right, well, we show them the way through the fairy door just like we did with you. Once they've settled in, if there isn't one already, we will ask the fairies to install one at the bottom of their garden or in a wood nearby if they live in a flat and get them back here via the scouts and it'll be like they've never been away."

Stanley planted his paw on his forehead with a sigh!

"I feel such a silly boy...thank you for explaining. It all makes sense now! I'm going back to the Comforter Wing to tell them!"

With that, he turned on his heels and ran all the way back to the Comforter Wing to tell the boys the good news!

Chapter 22

WHEN he got back, Maisie and the boys were delighted to see him as he told them all the things he'd discovered about Knowers. He kept the thing about "saying goodbye" to himself for a bit, he wanted to work it out in his own mind before he mentioned it to anyone else.

The boys were most impressed that he had gone into the Royal Chamber and spoken to the King and Queen like they were just any other tzus.

"Well Coffee found me and Bailey said we were friends so I became their friend. Is this a big deal then?"

The puppies all looked at him in amazement.

"What you just call them Coffee and Bailey?" said Brickie.

Stanley nodded.

"I call Coffee my Fosty Coffee," said Maisie!

"Wowser!" said Sammy "you two are like best pals of da most royal couple! I am in da presence of greatness!"

They all bowed and swept pretend hats of their heads and in front of their tummies.

Stanley and Maisie giggled at their new found fame!

Chapter 23

IT was certainly much quieter without the boys around in the Comforter Wing. Paddy, accompanied by Phoebe, had taken all the boys to Manchester in the end and carefully handed them over to Debs, the Knower.

Watching from the dog home's fairy door he waved at Debs as she took them away to safety and to find a new home. Knowers didn't know much, they knew enough to know that Paddy and the tzus were doing good work. She knew not to ask any questions and this is what made Knowers special – they just accepted things how they were and looked after the puppies that came their way. Paddy was a master at finding Knowers around the world, but Debs was definitely his favourite.

So, Paddy trusted Debs with puppies, she would find them all excellent homes and he would keep an eye on things from the Scout Tower until they were all in loving homes and he'd sniff them out as soon as they were settled so they could come to Tzu Kingdom and enjoy a tzu life too.

Caution dictated that Tzu Kingdom was a little too much to take in for puppies so the scouts usually waited until they were about 10 or 11 dog years old – just over one in human years - before they were shown the magic fairy doors and taught to bark loud and firm!

Paddy thoroughly enjoyed being a Scout and he was

so proud that Coffee referred to him as her 'second in command'. She had led the Scout Team for years, being so organised and efficient, but since she had married King Bailey a few years ago and become Queen and joint ruler, she had so much to do that someone had to step up so she could carry out her regal duties. One day soon, he hoped he would be appointed as Scout Team Leader and carry on her excellent work. He also wanted to expand the team, training scouts from an earlier age and making this a career that any young tzu would want to follow. His aim was to build a heroic team and his motto would be "...a warm paw extended to every known tzu" or "no tzu left behind" or something like that.

He also knew that would mean working more closely with Phoebe — Feebs - and the Rescuer Tzus and this made him smile. He thought she was amazing — fit, agile, clever and brave...he hadn't seen her for a few days because she had to look after her mum at home after an operation. She loved climbing up the Scout Tower with him to look at the view and hold paws. 'If she's not back tomorrow I'm gonna pop through her fairy door and surprise her,' he thought.

Paddy looked around Scout Tower and stood up tall as he thought that this may, one day in the future, be his domain. It was such a stunning building sitting right atop the Welcome Room. Accessed only by one of the four rope ladders and guarded by the tzus in the Welcome Room — although there was an emergency escape on the outside that had never been used. You needed a special bark sequence to get in here and it was passed down to just a few special tzus. It wasn't a place for puppies or elder tzus, although Paddy thought he might offer tours for young pups as part of his leadership and development programme one day.

The Scout Tower was the brainchild of King Romeo and his brother Nemo back in the human 1950s. Their human dad was a submariner and the brothers built the tower based on his nautical tails. The room was circular, in the shape of an observatory tower, clad with polished wood throughout. It was divided into North, South, East and West and at each corner was a telescope. By looking through the enchanted spy holes on each wall, they were able to see the entire Tzu Kingdom fairy door network across the world and carry out their essential job as scouts.

In the centre of the room was a small office where the lead scout kept all the paperwork on the fairy doors. Coffee sat here most of the time a few years ago, before she was Queen, and directed operations. Paddy found himself here more often now and enjoyed making quick fire decisions and rejoicing when they found a new tzu and opened up a new file. He didn't like the paperwork as much as Coffee though and, although it was up to date, he worried that she was doing too much and wondered if he might suggest that somefur could start helping out in the office a little more. He looked across the room to Bonnie and thought how good she would be at such a job.

He stopped daydreaming and looked back at his notes, still smiling, and ticked off the tzus that he had seen today. Mostly he had been doing his bi-annual check on the older tzus who, perhaps, they didn't see as much anymore, and it was sometimes his sad duty to report back a passing to Bailey and Coffee, something that required courage as much as rescuing did.

As he looked he realised, something was amiss.

He grabbed for the telescope and looked out West. The more he looked, the bigger the tzu gap became.

"Someone's missing" he said to himself and wrote a note with his pencil.

"Bonnie...Bonz, come and have a look in to Wales Door 371 for me would ya, something's not right is it?"

Bonnie stopped looking out through the looksie holes on the East wall of the Scout Tower and joined Paddy at his workstation.

Bonnie was pure white and quite dainty with extraordinarily long ears. She always wore sparkly clips in her ears to hold them back a little and to see clearly she would gather up both ears in her right front paw and hold them to the side to work. Paddy found this very cute.

"You're right Pads. Something is terribly wrong on the other side of that door."

Chapter 24

MEANWHILE, in the quiet of the Comforter Wing Maisie was asleep on Stanley who was asleep on a gigantic fluffy beanbag, having enjoyed some soup that Mabel and Myrtle had made that morning. Franc and Centime were on duty now and they were in the garden enjoying some cheese on the patio, basking in the sunshine.

The door swung open and there was Colin, looking quite distressed and holding up an elderly, and extremely dishevelled beige and white tzu.

"HELLO" shouted Colin and all four tzus ran to the entrance of the Comforter Wing to help him.

"I have a patient for you, I think."

"Who is this?" asked chocolate coloured Franc in his Parisian tones and knowing that this can't have been easy for Colin, with his limp and all.

"I'm not sure, she just turned up in the Welcome Room and, well, sort of collapsed on me. I just brought her straight here, I thought it best."

"You did the right thing Colin," said his adorably cute sister Centime, her long golden fur bouncing as she spoke in her soft, Parisian accent, and not drawing attention to his frailty.

"Bonjour, elegant lady, who are you, what is your name?" said Centime to the poorly dog in front of her.

Stanley thought what a polite thing this was to say

because the tzu didn't look elegant at all with her fur all knotted and full of twigs. She was in a sorry state and clearly needed some looking after. She had scratched her face quite badly and a lot of tail fur was missing. For Centime to be so considerate must have made her feel special because, underneath, he had no doubt she *was* an elegant lady.

"Where's Miss Coffee?" said the tzu. "Coffee, Coffee..."

"Do you mean Queen Coffee?" said Maisie.

"No, silly girl, of course not! Coffee is much too young to get married and Pierre is like a father to her!" she snapped.

Maisie felt embarrassed then she noticed that everyone was looking at each other funny. It wasn't a surprise – King Bailey had been on the throne of Tzu Kingdom for many dogs years now and Coffee had been his Queen for almost all that time. It was obvious that she didn't know that Old King Pierre had died and Bailey was the Tzu King now. Maisie realised that the elderly lady was confused, but she was still a bit upset about being spoken to sharply, especially when she was just trying to help.

"We will find Miss Coffee," said Centime, playing along, and looked at her brother. Franc nodded and ran off towards the Royal Chamber.

"Oh thank you sweet child," she said and, once again, collapsed. Colin and Stanley ran over to help and together they carried her on to a quilted bed in the girls' room where Centime covered her up with a soft blanket.

"I will get her something to eat from the kitchen" said Maisie and ran off to get some gentle broth. She had become so strong now that she was helping in the kitchen and feeling ever so useful and grown up indeed and she so wanted to help the elder, confused tzu, understanding what it is like to feel weak and unwell.

The elder tzu woke up again at the smell of the

delicious food from the Comforter Wing kitchen and smiled as she heard the familiar voice when Coffee entered the room.

"Oh my little poppet, it's really you!" she said as she sat up, paws outstretched.

"Nancy...my Nancy Noodle" said Coffee as she ran towards her friend jumped on the bed and cuddled her tightly.

Chapter 25

CENTIME swished her flowing golden locks in the direction of the Girls' Room door.

"Let us enjoy some croissants and preserve on zee patio," she said, and motioned for all the tzus to follow her. Of course they did, Centime might be tiny and quiet but without a doubt, she was a senior ranking tzu, the sister of much missed King Pierre, and she acted royally. You could see it – she just had an 'air of authority' about her. She spoke mainly French and when she tried to speak English, little words from her native country would slip in without her even noticing.

"Who is Nancy Noodle?" asked Colin once they got to the kitchen and Centime started to warm up delicious bakery treats and spoon gloopy strawberry jam into ramekins.

Centime sighed deeply and looked wistful as she started to tell Colin, Maisie and Stanley about Nancy.

"I only just remembers who she was, I recall from when I was a puppy and Franc and I had just settled in with King Pierre, Papa and Maman. She was not looking her best just now, we ladees will see to dis.

"Nancy hasn't been to Tzu Kingdom for some time, der is good reason for dis.... back many years ago, she was zee leader of zee Scouts. Coffee was her protégé and then her assistant, but most of all...she was her *meilleur ami*."

"What does that mean?" whispered Stan.

"Best friend." answered Colin. His dads were well travelled, he had a pet passport, and this made him quite the cosmopolitan dog-of-the-world, having been to France several times, as well as Belgium and the Isle of Wight. Maisie and Stan nodded.

"The scouts really found der *pattes* when Nancy and Coffee was in charge...."

"Paws." Colin whispered.

"Zee organisation was astounding. *De Tour de Scout* looked beautiful."

"Scout Tower." Colin was quite fancying himself as the competent translator now.

"Dey even introduced zee *telescopes.*"

"The telescopes," said Colin, helpfully. Stan glared at him. He could have worked that one out for himself. He didn't want Maisie thinking he was stupid. Colin blushed a little; he was only trying to be helpful.

"Nancy was zee model scout, she could see for da miles and miles through zee fairy door windows and spy a tzu like no one else....she was an inspiration to zee tzus. She was so much fun too...in her day, Pierre said, no one could keep up with her Paw Stomp. Oh and the hats....the shoes....the dresses....she and Coffee were such *fashionistas*....da trend setters in zee tzu world — der is photographs somewhere!

"Fashion...." Colin halted. That wasn't even French to translate.

"Nancy made it her life's work to find tzus-less-fortunate and one day she discovered a tzu so poorly that Pierre did not know if he would even make it back to zee Comforter Wing. Coffee was part of zee rescue mission and, thank goodness, she had big, strong Lennon with her to carry him home. Skin and bone, he could not bark, he was lifeless, he could not even open his eyes. My older brother thought all was lost but Coffee would not give up. She took time out from being a scout to nurse him night and day and, by some miracle, she saved his life.

"Pierre would tell this story to me and my younger brother often...zee story of love...zee story of how Coffee met Bailey."

Chapter 26

MAISIE was mesmerised by the love story of Coffee and Bailey that she had just heard. She loved the stories of Tzu Kingdom days gone by — Mabel and Myrtle were always telling tales of the old Kings and Queens from brave Leo to the first Queen, Sally, the rock star kings Groovy, Elvis and Bolan, beautiful and mysterious Queen Mirabelle, Pierre's mother, and Kindly King Hamish, who she fantasised was a forefur of her Stanley. She daydreamed about them as she ambled around the getting-better patio garden pretending she was a Princess or a Lady of the Court, swirling her skirts like a courtier's cloak, talking to her make-believe maid and enjoying imaginary banquets.

She was thinking that she would play a game of "Lady Maisie Rescues Prince Stanley" next week when he came for a visit when she saw someone standing in the doorway of the kitchen.

"Are you telling soppy tales Mademoiselle Centime?"

"Oh King Bailey, you made me jump high into zee sky!"

"I was telling zee young pups your story, yes, I cannot tell zee lies...I love zee romantical tale of our King and his Queen!"

Maisie felt a little bit awkward. She had been dreaming daft dreams and then here he was — Bailey himself. She thought about what Centime had told her and looked at the handsome dog she knew and couldn't believe he had known such bad times. Bailey was such a robust chap that she couldn't imagine him being thin and weak. Well, that's what love does for you, she thought.

It puzzled her still – how on earth did Bailey ever get in such a state? He was kind, thoughtful, wise and totally loveable.

For the first time in ages her mind wandered back to when she first met Stanley, Paddy and all the tzus and she felt a pang in her heart...she was a good dog too and she didn't deserve what she had at that horrible lady's house where it was cold and dirty. She started to wonder what would have happened to her if Paddy hadn't spotted her and come to her rescue with Stanley, Phoebe, Alice and Pom Pom that night. What if they hadn't escaped? What if Stanley had been caught...what if what if what if...

"Maisie...Maisie" Stan was shaking her. "What's the matter, you were whimpering and trembling."

"Oh Stan, I was just having a nasty day dream."

"Usually your daydreams are full of Lord and Ladies and Kings and Queens and I have to play at being your maid!"

Maisie giggled. "You're the bestest and I love you the mostest."

She jumped up into Stan's furry paws and nestled in to his tzu beard concluding that she loved playing her little courtier games and that she had a little romance all of her own. She was a lucky girl now and she knew it.

"Bailey says we are to go through to the Girls' Room. Coffee has brought Nancy up to date on all the tzu business and now, we have to put something right for her."

At that moment, they heard running pawsteps and they got louder and louder until they crashed through the Comforter Wing door. It was Paddy, followed by Bonnie.

"Stan...Maisie..." Paddy could hardly breathe. "We need King Bailey or Queen Coffee or both...he tried to take a breath and wheezed out a few more words.

"There's..... a senior tzu....in........mortal.....peril!"

Chapter 27

"HERE Paddy, have a sip of water." said Stanley, "would you like a croissant as well, steady yourself?" he asked.

"I think so Stan, for strength purposes. Perhaps a spoonful of jam on it, just for a bit of energy, you know, after the shock."

Stanley offered the same to Bonnie, although she didn't seem nearly as shaken as Paddy. She nibbled her croissant crescent neatly whilst Paddy gobbled his down in three bites, smothered in butter and dripping with jam. She honestly didn't know where he put it all.

Maisie tidied all the things away and wiped up the jam and swept the crumbs from the floor as Paddy, still with a little jam in his beard, started to explain.

"Bonz and me were in Scout Tower, on the evening shift, doing our regular checks on the elder tzus... everything was calm when I turned West and looked in to Wales. Everyone was accounted for, I ticked everyone on me sheet off one by one and then, I had a shock, something was amiss."

Bonnie piped up, "He called me over and asked me to take a look too and we saw, without any doubt, something was wrong, very wrong. An elder tzu had gone missing. We could see posters with a tzu photo and a phone number and we could hear her name being called frantically, and when we listened closely, a little human girl was crying."

Paddy continued."So, we had to raise the alarm. Bonz and me descended the West Tower rope ladder nose to tail and we ran here to report an emergency to the King and Queen."

"Thing is, it's not just any tzu, it's someone important in Scout Tzu history and we have to find her. It's Nancy, former Scout Leader and Coffee's best friend."

Stan and Maisie looked at each other and burst out laughing.

"It's not funny!" yelled Paddy and Bonnie together, pulling their angriest faces.

"Follow me..." said Maisie and scuttled towards the Girls' Room. She and Stan pushed the wooden door open and they laughed some more.

"Is this the Nancy you've misplaced?" said Maisie, smiling.

Chapter 28

PADDY could hardly believe his eyes. Nancy was like a legend amongst the scout tzus. Some remembered working with her, some remembered the "Coffee and Nancy Days". Most tzus knew that she was the one that found Bailey and ensured he was brought to the safety of Tzu Kingdom, where he would one day reign.

Colin had showed him one of his etchings recently, one of Coffee and Nancy dressed up for a Christmas party looking especially glamorous and here they both were in front of him — Coffee in one of her pretty long cardigans with a silk neckerchief and Nancy, well, looking like she had had a rough time with twigs in her tail, scratches and tear stains on her face.

He felt sadness come over him like a dark cloud and he reached out for Bonnie's paw.

'Brave as a lion. Brave as a lion.' he muttered under his breath as he felt the tears well up. Bonnie looked sad too, he squeezed her paw.

Coffee, of course, was quick to notice this and she jumped off the bed and took control. She was an awesome Queen.

"Tzus, we have work to do to put things right for Nancy. First of all Maisie, Centime, Bonnie could you jump up on the bed with Nancy Scout please and ensure she is comforted."

BOING. BOING. BOING.

The girls did just as they were told; they knew Coffee was nearly always right.

"Stanley, Paddy, Colin and Franc why don't you sit on a beanbag."

PLONK. PLONK. PLONK. PLONK.

The boys felt the same about Queen Coffee.

"Bailey darling..."

"I'm here by your side sweetpea."

"OK, so if I can please introduce to everyone my best friend from the olden days — Nancy."

Nancy waved at everyone and smiled, loving her newly re-discovered knowledge that her best friend was now the Queen of Tzus. She felt very special now, she had something worrying her that she hoped her friend would put right soon enough.

"Nancy was a big name in Tzu Kingdom once upon a time — as some of you know she was Chief Scout and, as well as teaching me everything I know, she found my darling Bailey for me. She also used to wear the most amazing outfits!

"As time rolled by, Nancy got older and retired from active duty and passed the stewardship of Scout Tower to me. Around this time, she was also sad to lose her human mother and has, since that day, been virtually dedicated to her wonderful human father, Ifan. She has barely left his side and this is the reason she has become a less frequent visitor to us here."

Nancy coughed and everyone turned to her.

"Well, Coffee my darling you are so sweet my love but, let's be honest...I'd completely forgotten about Tzu Kingdom in my ditsy old age until I saw that ancient tree and somehow I remembered to bark loud and firm and here I am and ....oh my Ifan, I hope he is OK without me..."

"Tzus" continued Coffee "somehow Ifan and Nancy

became separated and she stumbled across a communal fairy door in the park — you know, like tzus who live in flats and apartments use — and she barked loud and firm and landed in the Welcome Room...much to Colin's surprise!"

"We don't know quite what happened yet and this is why I am going to make a request of you Paddy."

Paddy's ears pricked up and he leapt up from the beanbag and stood to attention.

"Paddy, we must get Nancy home to her Ifan. He's an elderly gentleman and it is just the two of them in that big house and garden. I want you to go on a mission to check all is in order and that we can safely take Nancy home."

Paddy saluted.

"I shall leave at once my Queen Coffee, King Bailey and return Nancy in to Ifan's arms."

Chapter 29

PADDY loved an adventure and he was pleased to be taking such an active role in getting Nancy home to Ifan in Wales. He didn't want to be a rescuer himself, although he did love being chosen to go on a mission every now and then.

"What you lot going to do whilst I go on the mission then?" he asked.

"Well" said Coffee, "we can't let Nancy go home in such a bad way, poor Ifan just won't cope if he sees her like this so I thought we would all have a lovely pamper night here in the Comforter Wing and everyone can join in!

"We will have bubble baths, pawdicures, furcials and we will braid each other's fur and put cucumber slices on our eyes, clean ears, polish teeth...try new pawfumes..."

The girls squealed. Bailey looked forlorn.

"Oh, my darling, I wish I could but I have so much erm...King business to do...I mean loads....lots of thinking and jotting stuff down and...you know how it is".

"Oh darling," said Coffee, "what a shame...do you need help?"

"Oh, erm, I said I would help him," piped up Franc. "You know, in case Pierre ever told me something that he had forgotten to tell Bailey..."

"Oh, Franc, you are such a good tzu. Well, with Paddy on the rescue, that just leaves you two then here with us girls and all our lotions, potions and bath soaks..."

"Coffee, I would love to..." said Colin "but I have to go back and man the Welcome Room.

"Isn't Carmen there now? It's after six?"

"Oh, well, yes she *is* but she's been knitting puppy jumpers and her wool has gotten all tangled and I said I would help her straighten it out with my nimble paws."

"Well, that's very helpful of you Colin."

Bailey, Franc and Colin all ran out of the Comforter Room, holding their sniggers.

"So," continued Coffee, "I suppose if Paddy is off to check out Nancy's house then that just leaves you as the only boy on our pamper night Stanley. You had better grab a bathrobe..."

"Oh, I'm gonna need Stan I'm afraid QC. He has to come with me. Don't you remember Phoebe's new rules *"tzus must stay in pairs on rescues?"* I know it's not strictly a rescue but it could be dangerous — you never know."

"You are so right Paddy. How silly of me. Yes, Stan should go with you and check out how the valleys lie."

Once they were out of the room Paddy burst out laughing.

"Phew!" he said. "I side-swerved that one for you — you owe me a BIG favour!"

"What for?" asked Stanley "I thought a pampering sounded quite nice."

"Well, be my guest....go back in there....if you want to be smelling all froo froo and spend the night with your fur in....FURCURLERS!"

Paddy couldn't stop now — he was on his back snorting, giggling and waving his paws in the air with tears of laughter rolling down his cheeks and in to his ears.

"FURCURLERS! Oh my dog! Pads! You ARE a proper pal!" said Stanley, joining him in the giggle fest.

Chapter 30

COFFEE smiled as she listened to the boys scuttling away and laughing in the corridor outside.

"Well ladies, looks like my plan worked again!"

Centime and Bonnie both laughed and jumped off the bed. This wasn't the first time they had outwitted the boys and it wouldn't be the last. She had a twinkle in her eye — the Tzu Queen, whilst exemplary in her composure, could still be a mischievous little tzu every now and then. She had been a little "economic" with the truth over pamper nights.

Yes, it was true that there was pampering however, the girls were much more savvy than that.

Yes, there was fur braiding but that was just practical — Phoebe liked her fur to be tidy whilst she was rescuing. She couldn't have ear fur flying everywhere when she needed panoramic vision.

Yes, there were furcurlers, but Bonnie needed curls so she could put her clips in and see clearly out of the spyholes in Scout Tower.

Coffee herself, well, she had to set an example to all the young tzus and keep herself looking the part. It really was a tzu thing.

They would discuss important tzu stuff whilst they enjoyed their evening — things that affected tzus and the entire dog world. She mused that the boys had a very different view of Pamper Night to the one that actually happened!

There was nothing like a little bit of time with your girlfriends and the knack to making sure they had the whole evening together was to make them believe they were escaping something girly.

"I got zee message to Peeka" winked Centime and, with that, there was a knock at the door.

Peeka and Centime had become good friends recently; it was one day when Centime and Franc had been walking through Paris when they spotted Peeka with Madame outside the Moulin Rouge. Centime had never thought about where Peeka had learnt her dancing but it made sense when she explained that she worked there. Centime had always struggled with her English compared to Peeka who was almost fluent due to the tourists that visited all year around and she had taught Centime to a good standard.

"Can we come in?" said Phoebe, and in she walked with an assortment of tzus – Peeka, Alice, Pom Pom, Lola and Kiki.

"Hiya all" said Peeka "I have brought some cakes with me. We can have orange cake with lemon drizzle and lemon cake with orange drizzle, they are both as tasty as each other."

"Well hello ladies" said Coffee. Aren't we going to have a lovely evening now! Phoebe, is Mum better now?"

"Oh she is just fine thank you Coffee. Auntie is staying with us but there's nothing to worry about. She's all mended." she said, happily.

Coffee, Phoebe and the rest of the girls chatted away and plated up the cakes in the kitchen.

Eventually, they came back in to the room and saw a lovely sight. Young Maisie was snuggled up in elder tzu Nancy's arms, cuddling her precious teddy Millicent and listening to all the tales of Tzu Kingdom days gone by.

Chapter 31

MY first visit to Tzu Kingdom was in human year 1999, during the reign of King Hamish. He was a handsome chap; he was the colour of champagne, just like your Stanley. Scottish too. He would cut a dash on the dance floor in his kilt and tam o'shanter!

Hamish had ruled since 1991, the ruler before him had been his mother Queen Gypsophillia — a glossy long coated black and silver tzu who was responsible for the beautiful patio garden.

When we said goodbye to Hamish it was the saddest of days and the Kingdom was as sad as it could possibly be. Of course, the loss of any tzu is always sad, yet we have learnt to accept that every fur has their time.

Although, we never knew what became of King Wolfgang, who reigned during the humans' war. He was the Swiss King of Peace and he disappeared at the end of the war and, well, Queen Sally took over temporarily then, after a few months she was elected as Queen, on the understanding that she would rule equally with Wolfgang should he ever return, but that never happened. Sally was the ruler who introduced the Comforter Wing for the rescued, injured and unwell.

Next in the royal lineage was King Romeo — oh he was such a flirt! He was just the tonic Tzu Kingdom needed after the war and it was non-stop parties and romances back then! He was the one who built Scout Tower so he wasn't that bonkers!

After he nearly wore the Kingdom out, we had three

brothers consecutively on the throne — Groovy, Elvis
and Bolan. They were wild times and thank goodness
they had good advisors around them to keep things in
check! We all needed some fun and we were always
doing good throughout the craziness!

King Muffin was a quieter fellow, and lots of sensible
precautions were put in during his reign, such as the
safety staircase to Scout Tower and the Welcome Room
— things that Gypsophillia nurtured during her reign.

Then King Hamish, then Queen Mirabelle who added the
café to our world and, of course, the mother of King
Pierre.

And now King Bailey and Queen Coffee — a wonderful
ruling pair and the first to rule equally.

Chapter 32

MAISIE sighed and hugged Nancy tightly, completely forgetting that their first exchange had been a cross one. She understood that Nancy was confused then, and didn't know where or who she was. She scared Maisie a bit so it surprised her that she felt so completely differently about her now. She felt safe, fuzzy and warm with her, in a different way to the way she felt with Stanley, almost as if she had found a real tzu mummy to stroke her fur, kiss her nose and look after her. She wished that she could stay cuddled up with Nancy for always on the big bed.

"I love the Tzu Kingdom stories Nancy, I wish I wish I wish I knew what all the tzus from history look like. I think I will ask Mabel and Myrtle for a scrapbook and I can imagine them and then draw them and look at their pictures before I go to sleep at night."

"Why would you need to do that sweetheart when all their portraits are in Tzu Gallery?" asked Nancy, confused.

"Tzu what?" asked Maisie.

"Tzu Gallery, it's behind the big Party Room, where all the memories of Tzu Kingdom and the Tzus of days gone past are kept."

Maisie was confused then and she looked around at all the girl tzus that were sharing this lovely evening with her. Their doleful eyes showed that they knew what Nancy was talking about, but that none of them wanted to put it in to words.

Coffee looked up with sad eyes.

"It's locked Nancy; it has been since Colin was injured. Bailey just couldn't face it after Colin was hurt — he said he didn't measure up and he wanted to forget all about the gallery and all those forefurs he could never equal,"said Coffee.

Nancy shook her head slowly.

"So, Miss Coffee...then where are your wedding photos and your coronation paintings?"

"Well, we never had any coronation paintings and I just keep our wedding photo here, in my cardigan pocket. We eloped to Paris, you were my bridesmaid, remember?"

Out of her pocket, Coffee pulled a small Polaroid in which she beamed from long tzu ear to long tzu ear with an equally happy King Bailey next to her, his paws wrapped around her in the shadow of the Eiffel Tower. She smiled at the photo, stroked Bailey's beard in the image and showed it off to her friends, proudly.

"Oh, dear sweet Coffee," Nancy said haughtily, "I think I need to have a word with young Mr Bailey about this. You are an exceptional King and Queen and he must allow Tzu Kingdom and its inhabitants to celebrate this."

Centime butted in, "We all agree with you Nancy, but Bailey has never come to zee terms with losing Pierre or Colin's injury. He cannot accept zat Pierre had had his time or zat Colin is a happy tzu. He loves to be in zee Welcome Room and he is able to paint there too."

"He paints?" gasped Nancy. "Well, than I have an idea...but first we need someone small to find the key to the Gallery."

Maisie looked up. "I think this is a job for Millicent and me. We are a tzu and her bear and therefore... as brave as a lion and her cub!"

Chapter 33

COLIN was in the Welcome Room. By a somewhat unfortunate coincidence, Carmen actually did need some help unravelling some wool for making puppy jumpers when he got back and he found himself holding up a wonky green jumper whilst she unravelled it to where it had gone wrong.

Carmen had been a long time feature of Tzu Kingdom, enjoying the parties mostly in her younger days and helping out at the bar. She had turned to the Welcome Room recently because it gave her a calm and quiet place to knit. She wasn't terribly good at it, no matter how much she practised, but many a tzu was pleased to own one of her exclusive knitted creations if they decided to, unexpectedly, go skiing or snowboarding whilst there.

So, this wasn't the first time that Colin had found himself holding up a wonky jumper!

Maisie was thrilled to be going on an adventure with Millicent. Coffee insisted that she had to take Lola and Kiki for safety's sake. They planned it all meticulously, they would show her the way but the truly brave part – finding the key – was all down to baby tzu and bear. She hadn't been out of the Comforter Wing very much since she had arrived and, Phoebe explained, you can feel very brave when you are somewhere safe yet it's different when you venture out, especially after being poorly. They let her go ahead alone from where they could see her in the corridor, knowing that she needed to build her tzu confidence up. She had dressed for the occasion too, wearing a smart tracksuit for adventures. Pink, of course. Nancy had advised her on what to wear.

She watched cautiously from the corridor, at first, sizing up the room hiding her face behind Millicent so she felt almost invisible.

Nancy and Coffee had talked it through and felt sure that King Bailey would have hidden the key in the Welcome Room and that it was just a case of slipping past whosoever was on duty. The rest of the girls had discussed the rota and figured out that it was most probably Carmen and, so, there probably would be some sort of knitting related incident of chaos under way. Of course, she wouldn't miss any swooshes or any gassy tzus arriving through a fairy door, however, she was unlikely to pay much attention to the corridors.

Maisie's eyes were wide with excitement as she surveyed the Welcome Room. It was an assortment of colourful bean bags and cushioned chairs, long velvet curtains with tassels, bowls of water and trays of biscuits. She began to put everything in Tzu Kingdom into context – the four entrances to the Scout Tower, the Party Room, the corridor to the Royal Chamber and the magical doors that led back to everyone's homes.

It was much bigger than she thought it would be and she started to feel a bit scared that she would get it wrong. She turned back to her friends and they somehow sensed that she was having a wobble.

"She's gonna bottle it," said Kiki.

"We can't let that happen. Follow my lead!" said Lola.

Lola fluffed out the fur around her face and Kiki followed suit, knowing what they were going to do.

They stood up tall and made themselves look like lions, silently roaring and waving their paws encouragingly.

Maisie stifled a giggle in to Millicent. They had her

back. Having friends was a marvellous thing.

'Where are the keys?' Maisie mimed to them by shrugging her shoulders and turning an air key in a pretend lock.

'In the desk drawer' mimed Kiki, pretending to be a desk whilst Lola pulled out a pretend drawer and picked out a pretend bunch of keys and waved them in the air.

Maisie couldn't believe her luck when she turned back into the circular room to look for the desk. She could see the back of Colin sitting on a chair holding up a green jumper that, she thought, may be being knitted for an octopus with all those paw holes and sleeves. She could only hear an elder lady tzu on the other side, reading out from a pattern book and muttering to herself.

"This is our chance Millicent," she said.

Being so tiny, she made very little noise and she scuttled to the desk and squeezed in behind Colin. Quietly, she opened the bottom drawer but no luck; it was full of notebooks, bows and buttons. The middle drawer was no better; it was full of ledgers and dust.

'Fiddlesticks!' she thought. 'I can only just reach the huge top drawer and I will have to stand on Millicent to do that.' Luckily, her teddy was always happy to oblige.

Up she climbed on Millicent until her nose was just above the top of the drawer. She eased it open as gently as she could until she could peer in with ease and what she saw inside was a delight for the girl who loved her stories of old.

There were paintings, drawings and photographs of tzus, stuffed in on top of each other. Some were old, tinged with sepia and faded with age, some were in frames that had disintegrated over time and some were brand new, as if the paint had just dried.

She gasped in awe and then clasped her paw to her mouth, knowing she had to be silent.

For a moment, she almost forgot what she was looking for until, that is, she saw an old rusty key on a chain, weighing down all the photographs. She grabbed it, hoping this was the key that led to Tzu Gallery and jumped down off Millicent, ready to scarper back to Kiki and Lola when she felt a paw on her shoulder.

"What you doing Maisie Moo?" said Colin, in the softest of whispers, with his good back leg still on her.

Maisie couldn't think of a believable cover story. She had Millicent in one paw and a key in the other. She had to be as brave as a lion and tell the truth.

"We want to open up Tzu Gallery.....for King Bailey and, well, well that's it really," she murmured, biting her lip when she had finished.

"Me too! It's been my dream!"

"Let's plan it...tomorrow?!" enquired Maisie.

"OK, when Stan and Paddy are back and your froo froo Pamper Night with furcurlers is safely out of the way!" sniggered Colin, turning back to the enormous green jumper and Carmen's confusion.

Chapter 34

IN Wales, two little boy tzus were also on their tip paws as they landed in the garden that was home to Nancy and her beloved human dad, Ifan. They sought refuge behind the tree that was the link between a home and Tzu Kingdom, a beautiful fairy door twinkling in the evening sunshine.

Paddy briefed Stanley on the operation.

"Right, it's simple. All we need to do is assess things here, check Ifan is ok, and then slip Nancy back through the fairy door. We'll have her back for bedtime biscuits and no mistake."

"Right you are!" Stanley replied. "Shall we just get a little bit closer and peer in, see if he's ok."

"Good idea Stanley."

Paddy nodded enthusiastically, realising that Stan was an intelligent fella and good to have on your side. They tip-pawed from tree to tree, closer and closer to the house.

The closer they got, the less and less it seemed right.

"I don't think much of these garden ornament Pads, they are not pretty like the ones in my garden in Edinburgh. Maybe things are different in Wales but these just look like square blocks."

"They're bricks Stan," he replied. "Big grey house bricks and they are all dusty and it's getting in my eyes and they're hurty."

The boys lost concentration for a moment as they licked their paws and rubbed their eyes. It was making them sore and they weren't as organised as Coffee with her handkerchiefs, so it just made them worse.

All of a sudden, with no warning, out of the misty brick dust they heard the tring of a bell and a wheeled monster with a basket for a nose and two eyes on stalks came trundling towards them.

"STRANGER DANGER! RUN! ABANDON MISSION!" yelled Paddy, grabbed Stanley's paw and ran in his helter skelter fashion until they were back behind the tree, squashed up against a painted green shed.

"What's going on?" said Stan, feeling extraordinarily scared. This wasn't feeling like a simple job anymore and he wished Coffee or Bailey were around to ask. He was starting to get scared that he would never get back to Mama and Daddy with it all going so horribly wrong and a monster after them.

Paddy shook his head and hid his face in his paws. He took a deep breath.

"That's a human riding that monster Stan, it's called a bike and, what's more, it's not Ifan or anyone we know. There's only one explanation. Nancy is alone in this world. Ifan's dead."

Chapter 35

IF Stanley had learnt a few things about his friend Paddy, it was that he did, occasionally, get a bit carried away, somewhat over-excited with a bit of a tendency to leap to the most dramatic of conclusions.

That was fine of course, because everyone has their foibles and accepting those about your friends was a big part of being a friend. But he did consider it might not be a bad idea to try to get Paddy's paws back on the floor and look at some other possible explanations, although he feared his pal might be correct.

"Paddy, just bear with me here and maybe we could think this through...see if there is another reason for the monster to be in Ifan and Nancy's garden.

"I mean, do you think they might be visitors?"

Paddy shook his head again and sighed. "They might be Stan the Man, but that don't explain the bricks."

He had a point.

"Do you think Ifan might have moved?" Stanley had lived in a flat when he was a puppy, consequently he knew all about moving houses.

"He wouldn't go anywhere without Nancy. No, they love this house, I mean, look at it. Anyway, there's been no "For Sale" sign, boxes or packing up that I've seen."

Stan had to admit, it was very pleasant, although not as nice as his own home he thought.

He couldn't think of any other reasons, apart from the one that Paddy had already outlined.

"Nancy...Nancy... is that you?" called the voice of a little human girl.

"Cripes...the Monster Rider has seen us! Back through the fairy door...."

It was too late. The little girl was kneeling on the floor right next to them — they were cornered.

Chapter 36

THE Monster Rider looked at the boys. They grimaced, not sure what to do at all. Yet, the girl didn't seem that scary. She had long brown hair tied back with a yellow hair band and blue jeans with a long sleeved green t-shirt and a pink poncho. It didn't match really, but in a funny sort of way it did. She had style and certainly not monster style.

"Oh, you two aren't Nancy" she said, and started to cry. The two friends warmed to her straight away.

"You know Nancy?" barked Stanley, forgetting that humans couldn't understand Tzu.

"Yes, I'm Fleur and I live here and she's Grandpop Ifan's dog and she looks like your friend but smaller and more grey and a bit wobbly," she snivelled, wiping her eyes with her sleeves "she's gone missing and Grandpop Ifan is in hospital because he fell over, and he will never talk to Mummy, my little sister Skye or me again if we can't find her because he loves her so much but it wasn't our fault. We have just moved back from Germany where Mummy was working and we are moving in here to the house because Grandpop Ifan is old and poorly and not coping and we are building a Grandpops Annexe with no stairs for him and Nancy to live in and a door through to us and the builders left the gate open and Nancy wandered off and we haven't seen her for two days and Grandpop Ifan is coming home tomorrow and Mummy thinks he won't get better if he hasn't got Nancy anymore and...and...

and....I love Nancy too and I miss her soooooo much it hurts.....and...and...."

She started to cry uncontrollably. Paddy realised, he had heard a little girl crying yesterday and loudly too – it all made sense – and the best news was that Ifan wasn't dead after all, thank goodness, he was just in hospital. What was even better is that they weren't going to be on their own any more, his grown up daughter was coming to live with them so she could take care of them and bringing kind little tzu-loving humans with her. It was better than he could have hoped for for Nancy.

"It's OK, she's safe, little girl, she's with us and we are going to bring her home to you," said Paddy.

The crying stopped immediately and she flung her arms around them both.

"Hold on a biscuit-begging minute," said Stanley, "how comes you can hear what we say in words and not woofs?"

Fleur shrugged her shoulders, she didn't know. She couldn't remember a time when she'd actually had a conversation with Nancy after all.

"Oh wow! This is amazing," said Paddy, "it's never happened to me, but Coffee said it happened to Nancy once."

He shook his head; he just couldn't believe their luck.

"You see Stan, humans can sometimes understand us. It usually happens when we're enchanted; you know when we come through the fairy doors and get home, at least for the first few minutes."

"But Paddy, my Mama can't understand me when I come back?" Stanley remarked, quite confused.

"Oh, it's just something that happens to little humans, well just a few of them...clever ones that are in tune with animals and fairies and stuff like that. They seem to grow out of it when they get older and they forget to listen and look properly, clogging their heads up with music and games and jobs and responsibilities. They don't all *completely* forget, some of them grow up to be rescuers and knowers like my Debs in Manchester where we took the four boys."

"Excuse me Paddy? Stan? Can Nancy come home then?"

She looked at them with hope in her eyes and Paddy smiled broadly. It looked like things were going to work out perfectly.

"Yes...Fleur..? But we can't have your mum or sister cottoning on to this, so we have got to hatch a plan very quickly, before the enchantment wears off..."

Chapter 37

PADDY spoke faster than normal as he masterminded a plan to get Nancy home to Fleur and Ifan without raising any suspicions.

Fleur had explained that Grandpop Ifan was due home tomorrow afternoon and that she and Skye left for school at about a quarter past eight in the morning and that she was due a bath and bedtime very shortly.

"Well, it doesn't make any sense to get Nancy home tonight because you are gonna have your bath and your mum won't hear anything and, anyway, she's being pampered by all her girlfriends..."

"...and Paddy and I would rather not interrupt that because of all the pawfume and fur curling," piped up Stanley.

They both laughed. Fleur giggled too.

"Sshhhh," said Paddy, "don't say too much Stan," as they both remembered they should be keeping these things secret.

They carried on planning and deciding the best way to get Nancy back safely into the garden without giving anything about Tzu Kingdom away. Fleur could be trusted – they had no doubt about that – and Paddy knew that no one would believe her if she started talking about talking dogs anyhow.

Nancy would be brought through the fairy door at about 7am and she, and the tzu who would accompany her, would bark really loudly. Fleur would get up early and look out of the kitchen window. Once she was sure she had seen them, she would wave at the accompanying tzu and holler to her mum that Nancy was in the garden and they would run out and collect her.

Fleur would set her alarm, although no one thought she would sleep very much tonight.

"One of the rescuer Tzus will bring her home, probably Tanner, and she will be all safe and sound and looking all froo froo I'm sure."

Fleur was profoundly excited.

"Oh thank you Paddy and thank you Stanley — you are wonderful and I love you," she hugged them again, "I wish you could come and live with us all...Mummy already said we can get more dogs now we are back in Wales."

"Thank you Fleur although that is a nice offer, I have Mama and Daddy in Scotland and I live with them" said Stanley, with a little bit of panic in his eyes at the thought of living anywhere else bar with them.

"...and I live with me Mam, Dad and Mitch in Belfast," said Paddy.

"Oh you both look like you have the best homes, I was just saying...will I ever see you two again?" she asked.

"Well, I don't know, it would be nice to pop in and see Nancy...." Paddy noticed that Fleur was shaking her head and looking confused.

"I can only hear woofs now." she said.

Chapter 38

STANLEY snored so loudly that he woke himself up with a start. He looked around and realised he had been deeply asleep in his basket in Mama's office.

"Hello my little man! You've slept all day. We've not had a peep out of you since breakfast. Daddy will be home soon," she said as she picked him up and hugged him tightly.

"Oh Stanners, I have just been reading a story about an elderly shih tzu who got lost but it's **OK**, it has a happy end."

He looked at her seriously, very much hoping that it did.

"Her daddy was in hospital getting a new hip and she was home with her daddy's adult daughter and her two little girls. Whilst he was away the builders left the gate open and she wandered off. She's very old you see and they were doing everything to find her. They put posters up everywhere, put her on Doglost, adverts in the newspaper, went on the radio and started asking everyone on Twitter and Facebook."

There was something about this story that started to sound particularly familiar to Stanley.

"So, the poor little tzu, she was missing for three long nights and then...would you believe it...on the very day her dad was due to come home from hospital she just turned up in the back garden. His granddaughter Fleur just found her there..."

'*Really?*' He thought, trying to look surprised, his eyebrows raised to the top of his head.

"She's called Nancy, she's 18 in human years."

'**Nancy you say?**' thought Stanley, with his eyebrows almost to the ceiling.

"But here's the oddest thing. She had been bathed, brushed and smelt of raspberry shampoo with all her fur curly. I can't imagine what happened there."

'**Me neither!**' thought Stanley, smiling to himself, eyebrows almost to the chimney.

"Oh Stanners" said Mama, kissing his fur time and time again "thank goodness she's home and the family is all back together and Nancy is safe. I couldn't imagine not knowing where you were for a minute, I love you so much."

Over Mama's shoulder he looked at her computer screen and he couldn't have been happier. There was Fleur, with a smiling Grandpop Ifan, her mummy and sister cuddling his friend Nancy the elder tzu, and she looked stunning following her evening with the fur curlers and the tzu ladies.

I have the **BEST** of both worlds he thought and snuggled in to his mother, until it was time to wait at the door for Daddy.

Chapter 39

BORED BORED BORED.

Maisie was the most bored she had ever been.

After the whirlwind excitement of Nancy's visit, apart from a visit from Colin at which they shared a bowl of soup and spoke about Tzu Gallery, nothing particularly fun had even tried to happen.

Getting Nancy home had been brilliant though — right in the middle of pamper night, after Maisie had returned with the Tzu Gallery key and just as they were massaging and tidying up Nancy's paws- Stan and Paddy had scurried back in to the Comforter Wing at triple speed and gabbled on and on about Ifan, the bricks, the monster that turned out to be Fleur and, most exciting of all, the fact that Fleur could understand them for a little bit.

Phoebe ran off to get King Bailey and Franc and when they came back, conversation had already turned to the tactical plans of getting Nancy back to Fleur and Ifan.

King Bailey was deeply happy — he loved it when things went to plan and he could not stop commending Paddy and Stan for their bravery and quick thinking and, even better, they had been smart enough to plan how to return a tzu to her home before the enchantment wore off and Fleur could no longer understand them. He was very proud of them both.

The morning was going to be very exciting and Bailey

and Coffee decided to put a senior rescuer on the reunite mission. It was a safe one, so it was decided that the very experienced Tanner would take her through alone. Mac, the scout who would be on duty in the morning, would keep watch from Scout Tower, just in case of anything unexpected cropping up.

With the lateness of the hour, sleepy tzus started to say their goodnights and go home. Franc and Centime would shortly return to Paris accompanied by little Peeka, Paddy scampered back to Belfast and Phoebe to New York. One by one, they all went home, cuddling everyone goodbye and arranging to meet up before not too long and checking they had the date of the next tzu party in their heads too, it wasn't that far away now.

Stan hugged Maisie tightly.

"I will see you in a few days my lovely girl. Mama has to go on a business trip to London and Daddy works long hours so I have to go and take care of Granny. I will see you when I get back to my house."

"I understand Stan, I will think of you every moment until you get back" she said as she kissed him goodnight.

It really was love.

The reunite went absolutely according to plan. At 6.45am, Tanner met Nancy in the Comforter Wing as Mabel and Myrtle arrived. The ladies wished her well, quickly fussed and brushed her fur through once more and waved her off at the door telling her not to leave it too long to return this time, especially as it looked as though she didn't have quite as much responsibility to shoulder by herself now.

"Sure I will...!" said a smiling Nancy as she headed off down the corridor with a swishing tail following Tanner and holding paws with Maisie who had been allowed to go with them and say goodbye on condition that she was good as gold and did everything Tanner said without question.

At the Welcome Room she kissed Nancy goodbye whilst Tanner woofed the fairy door open.

"You will come back won't you?" said Maisie, a little tearful.

Nancy stroked her long curly ears and bomped her nose with her paw.

"Oh my little one of course I will...I don't have to watch over Ifan all by myself now and Megan, Skye and Fleur are lovely so they will help me all the time and I can have some 'me time' and come through as often as I want to."

"And I promise you something – if you keep the key to Tzu Gallery safe, I will come back in a few days and we will go through and look at what we can do to restore it to its former glory and do something really special for Coffee and Bailey."

"Do we have a deal?" she spoke, in a mummy-like fashion.

Maisie nodded and grinned – "DEAL!"

They had a big squeeze and Maisie thought how sensational and smart she looked after Pamper Night.

"Come on Nancy, time to go home to your loving family," said a deep and velvet-voiced Tanner, "wait here little Maisie, I shall be back in a few minutes."

Tanner woofed again, loud and firm and a fairy door opened wide, they jumped through, leaving Maisie standing on her own.

She looked over to the welcome desk and saw a tiny cream and beige coloured tzu wearing an enormous bonnet. They waved at each other. Maisie looked around again at the beanbags and sofas that adorned the room and thought how lucky she was to be a Shih Tzu.

To the left of the desk she could see through to the café lounge where there was a bustling and brisk trade in morning as teas, juices and bacon rolls were served to tzus of all shapes and sizes whilst they were chatting, laughing or napping on the chairs, sofas and beanbags. There were so many different coloured tzus, an assorted mix of voices and subtle differences that made her breed unique. She spied a couple of tzus with just one eye and a lovely brown tzu with a missing front leg. She wondered what had happened to them in their lives and vowed to come back and meet them one morning and hear their tales.

With that, there was a swoosh, a bump and a deep, loud and lengthy burp! Tanner was back. Maisie giggled at his burp.

"That was a piece of cake!" he said, "Fleur was waiting there on her bike just like she arranged with the boys; she gasped when she saw Nancy and scooped her up in her arms and nuzzled in to her fur. Nancy was wagging her tail like a puppy! She said thank you and ran back to the house shouting for her mummy. It was lovely! I wish every mission was like that". Tanner looked wistful, thinking of a rescue he'd be running soon that was going to test him and Phoebe to their limits.

"And Ifan will be back soon so it will all be ok!" said Maisie, happy with this news and blissfully unaware of the matter that was worrying Tanner.

"Of course it will — and that is one BIG house that she lives in, even without the Grandpops Annexe! Come on little one, back to the Comforter Wing with you, I promised those sisters I would get you back and, anyway, I have to have a catch up with my rescue team. There's a big operation planned in the next few days, top secret!" he tapped the side of his nose with his paw.

Maisie was about to ask what the secret operation was when with a whoosh and a burp, Phoebe landed to their right with gracefulness and a quiet pop of a burp.

"Morning everyone," she said, straightening up her notepad and pencil, "you ready for our meeting Tanner?" she asked the handsome rescuer.

"Sure thing Lady Feebs!" he answered and they both bid Maisie their "see you laters friend" as they ushered in to the corridor to the Comforter Wing and went into the café.

And so Maisie had been back in the Girls Room ever since, on her own. Thing is, she felt remarkably well now and she didn't feel that she needed to wear her pyjamas or be in bed all day and she was eating well too. Her whole puppy life she had felt cold and poorly and, well, she supposed that the way she felt now was what it felt like to be a well girl.

A bored one.

Mabel and Myrtle were sleeping in their rocking chairs, snoring away in the tzu fashion and no one else she knew was around.

She thought it was time to take a little wander around Tzu Kingdom by herself because she, Maisie, was also brave as a lion now.

Chapter 40

MAISIE tip-pawed past the sleeping Comforters and pushed the big wooden door open as quietly as she could. She shut it, slowly, behind her and started skipping down the very same corridor that Coffee had carried her down on the night she had arrived all those weeks ago.

She looked down at her paws, remembering how grubby they were back then. They were almost pure white now and they smelt of fruit and flowers. She also noticed that she didn't wobble on her legs any more as she walked even though there was a lot more of her now – her posture was tall and straight and her tail swished from side to side as much as her fur – now grown back silky and long – bounced up and down as she walked.

She had taken to wearing furclips with bows at the top of her ears and Stanley thought they looked adorable and cute, which was a nice thing to say, but she liked to balance the adorability with a denim jacket to show she was a tough little girl too.

She arrived at the Welcome Room to see the same little beige tzu she saw when Nancy had gone back with Tanner.

"Hello" said Maisie, shyly and bravely

"Hi there little one, you must be Maisie. I'm Zena... do you like my hat?"

"It's amazing, it's huge!" she said, wondering how she

even kept it balanced on her head.

"What you up to Maisie? Did Mabel and Myrtle send you for something?"

"Oh yes" she said, telling a little white lie and thinking on her paws. "They want me to check the floor has been swept for the party next week."

"Oh super, I can't wait for the party and to meet all the new tzus the scouts have found. This will be your first proper one won't it? I hear those four cheeky boys are coming back with Manchester accents to boot! They all have new families you know, they went off in pairs I think — just like Paddy hoped. Go on then, through you go."

This made Maisie smile, she couldn't wait to see her friends again and she hoped they would all be able to play and dance the "Paw Stomp" together. She had been practising it every day and had her stomps almost perfect now and couldn't wait to dance to the live band, although Stan and Paddy had been very good at the singing when they were rehearsing in the Comforter Wing. Phoebe was a great Paw Stomper too — she just had a knack for dancing, especially with Paddy.

So, she moseyed in to the Party Room and stared. It was everything she had dreamed of even though there wasn't even a party going on.

The main Party Room had a cosmopolitan bar as well as a stunning dance floor that lit up like a rainbow when you strode on to it and twinkling fairy lights hung from corner to corner all around. There were little cupboards, clearly labelled, around the perimeter with indicators for things like "*dancing boots*", "*party clothes*", "*beachwear*" and "*hats*".

On a large stage with swishy deep red curtains there was a drum kit, a sparkling piano and guitars of every colour, as well as tambourines and a microphone. On the big drum was written "Tzu Aroo".

There were sets of closed double doors that had

signs for all sorts of activities that said *"Beach"*, *"Ski Slopes"* and *"Team Sports"* and underneath each was written *"Please ask for the key at the Welcome Room"*.

She could not wait to see the party in full swing and for everything to come alive. Then she noticed another set of doors right at the back of the hall, covered by a pair of long, forbidding-looking, floor-length black curtains. She ventured over and poked her nose through them. She stood on her tip paws and read the sign.

"NO ADMITTANCE AT ANY TIME by order of King Bailey" it said, which Maisie thought was very out of step with everything else in Tzu Kingdom. She put her paw in her pocket and it dawned on her.

She had found Tzu Gallery.

She looked at the key in her paws – would it fit? Well, there was only one way to find out. Gingerly, she put it in to the keyhole, it was stiff but, with all her tzu strength, she managed to turn it and the door was unlocked.

She really didn't know what to do then because her Nancy had promised to take her in there and she wasn't sure that going in alone was doing the right thing, but curiosity got the better of her. She turned the door handle and opened the door, just a smidgen, and pushed her nose through the gap. It was dark and dusty – she sneezed – when she opened her eyes she could make out portraits of Kings and Queens in the room, hanging sad, wonky and unloved under redundant spotlights.

A big spider ran across one of the paintings and that made her slam the door shut and scream! She took a deep breath. She didn't really like spiders and she felt a bit hot and flustered whilst she regained her composure.

'I can't do this on my own' she thought, locking up again, 'and it would be naughty to go without Nancy because I said I would wait for her to come back to go in here. This needs a team — that's the way of Tzu Kingdom — and I need Nancy to help right now.'

She scampered back through the Party Room and in to the Welcome Room, right to the Fairy Door Wall.

"I want to see Nancy" she barked quite firmly and, to her complete surprise, a door opened wide enough for her to jump through. And so she did.

Just as a burpy Stanley arrived through another door.

Chapter 41

MAMA had arrived back early from her business trip last night and had picked Stanley up early morning from Granny's. She had missed him, obviously, so she changed her train to an earlier one to come home for cuddles. Stanley was ecstatic when he saw her — Granny hadn't even told him because she thought it would be a fantastic surprise for the little vanilla one when she walked through the door, unexpectedly.

He was a teensy bit sad, because he always got extra treats from Granny as they snuggled up on their early "telly and knitting in bed" nights but, he would be back soon another day.

Mama was busy when they got home, sorting out orders from her trip, so when she took a tea break on the decking, he popped down to the fairy door. It was jolly nice to have a surprise that he thought he would "pass it forward" and surprise his little Maisie pops. On the way to the tree, he stopped and picked her a bunch of dandelion clocks, knowing she would love and treasure them.

He landed with his usual bump, burp and pardon. The burps still made him laugh as he came through the fairy door each time, even though he should be used to it. Not everyone said pardon, as they were so accustomed to it that burping didn't seem to be a big deal. But to him, burping was always funny.

He skipped along the corridor to the Comforter Wing and paused at the door to check the dandelion clocks were alright and to smooth down his beard, check he didn't have any dog biscuit crumbs in his teeth or fur, and to fluff his tail plume.

He pushed open the door and looked to see where everyone was. Mabel and Myrtle were fast asleep and snoring in their rocking chairs. According to the board, there was still only one in-patient and that was his Maisie. He went straight to the room and knocked on the door, she didn't answer so he kept knocking and opening the door slowly.

Concluding that she must be asleep, he finally poked his head around the door. He still couldn't see Maisie, but Millicent the teddy bear was propped up the bed, on top of her folded up pyjamas and leaning on a plump pink cushion with feathers.

Well, thought Stan, she never goes anywhere without Millicent so she must be here but, after he had looked under the bed, in the wardrobe and in all the nooks and crannies, she was still nowhere to be seen and he felt a little bit panicky. There was nothing else for it, he would have to wake up the sisters and ask where she was hiding.

"Mabel and Myrtle," he said, tugging at both their aprons, because he still couldn't tell them apart, "where's Maisie please?"

They both jumped and snorted as they woke.

"Stanley pudding pie," said Mabel or Myrtle, "what's up?"

He explained that he couldn't find Maisie and they jumped up, sniffing the air.

"Well, it smells like someone's gone on a little adventure," one of them said, looking towards the corridor.

"WHAT?" said Stanley, with wide eyes; his heart feeling like it was in his throat.

"Stanley it's OK, she'll be fine. She's a lot better than she was when she first came here — haven't you noticed how she's stopped wearing her jimjams and sleeping all day and night? She's better! In fact, we were only talking with our little Miss Coffee Cup yesterday about trying to find her a home."

"A home? You mean, away from Tzu Kingdom?"

"Darling Stanley Pudding, she can't live here permanently. We are here to make poorly tzus better and then find them the perfect home for the rest of their lives. You remember?"

He did remember this conversation, he had pushed it to the far corner of his mind because he didn't like to think of her not being here when he came through every time. Sure, he had quite a few friends in Tzu Kingdom but, well, she was his girl and he loved spending time with her.

Mabel and Myrtle seemed to pick up on his disappointment, maybe because the dandelion clocks were now trailing on the floor by his feet. One of the sisters put her paw under his chin and nudged his head to look up at her.

"Chin up young man! Where's that brave little lion dog, hmm? Maisie will still come through loads and you can arrange times to meet up with her too. You two are devoted to each other and that never has to change, it just gets a bit more grown up and you both have to be organised."

He smiled because she was right but then he remembered he still didn't know where she was. He opened his mouth to speak...

"If you want to find her, then you need to employ that little tzu button nose and sniff her out! Pick up her scent and follow it, we've both got a fairly good idea where she might be!"

The sister tapped his nose and smiled, lovingly, at him.

"Well, sniffing time it is then!" giggled Stanley.

Chapter 42

SNIFFING was a lot of fun and, after he had left the dandelion clocks in a vase by Maisie's bed, he followed her scent all the way down the corridor, in to the Welcome Room and off to the Party Room. It took him right to the back, past lots of doors and a big black set of curtains and right up to an old lock in a wooden door. Then, to Stanley's surprise he followed it back down to the Party Room and then to the Welcome Room, feeling like he'd been on a bit of a wild goose chase.

The scent stopped at the Fairy Door Wall, where the feelings of worry returned when he was aware that there was someone behind him. It was Zena, one of the Welcome Room tzus.

"Stanley pup, are you looking for your Maisie?" she said, in a most friendly manner.

"Yep!" he said, feeling a bit happier.

"Oh, she went to see her Nancy, I watched her jump through. We were pretty sure that she would venture after her before too long! They really have bonded those two haven't they?"

Stanley nodded, he had to agree. It was like they were mummy and daughter.

"Will she be able to get back?" he asked her.

"Oh, I would think so, but shall I call up to Paddy? He's up in Scout Tower keeping an eye on her I don't doubt!"

"Yes please Zena."

Zena scampered back to her desk and picked up a Bakelite telephone. Stanley could hear it ringing at the other end.

"Scout Tower." said Paddy's voice through the telephone. Stan was excited to hear him; he could really do with a friend right now.

"Welcome Room here Mr Paddy. I have young Stanley the vanilla tzu down here and he's enquiring about Maisie, his girlfriend."

Stanley blushed at the 'girlfriend' word.

"Oh send him up the north rope ladder, that's the easiest one to climb, just tell him to be careful, concentrate, and I shall meet him at the top."

The excitement of seeing Scout Tower was almost too much for Stanley and he ran towards the door to the north. He heard Paddy bark a special sequence and a door opened to reveal one sturdy rope ladder for him to climb.

Up and up he went, clinging on to the rope ladder with his sharp claws. It was ever such a long way up and he was feeling a little dizzy as he got nearer to the top.

"Don't look down, just follow my voice Stan..." hollered Paddy.

He followed his pal's instructions until he saw a black and white paw extended to him at the top of the ladder. He grabbed it and jumped the final few steps straight in to Paddy's outstretched paws.

"Gotcha!" said Paddy. "Welcome to Scout Tower."

Chapter 43

THE views from Scout Tower were breath taking and Stanley knew about views — from his garden he could see Edinburgh Castle after all — but he didn't know if that, or the inside of Scout Tower, was the most impressive.

He marvelled in awe at the wooden panelling, the brass wheels, spy holes and nautical décor throughout. In the middle, the circular desk was a treat in anyone's eyes and his very own pal — Paddy — was sat right in the middle, swirling around on a large leather chair.

"Wotcha think?" he said, stopping his swirl with his back paws pressed on the oak control desk that dominated the centre of the room.

"It's incredible," said Stan.

"Take a look through a scope," he said, "I've been watching little Maisie through the West scope, it's trained on Nancy's garden. She's fine! They are playing hide and seek around them bricks we was scared of!"

Stanley looked through the telescope and there she was - happy with Nancy in the garden. Suddenly, an exciting thought popped in to his head.

"Paddy, the senior lady tzus have been talking about Maisie's forever home. I was just thinking, do you remember when we met Fleur and she said that her mummy was thinking about getting more doggies? Well, might it not be the best idea ever if she was to live with Nancy? After all, the house is massive and there is such a lot of love there and she would have Fleur, her mum, Skye and Ifan as well as Nancy..."

Paddy leaned back in his chair, he was laughing to himself.

"You're not the only tzu to think that Stan...Coffee and Bailey mentioned it to me the other day. We need Maisie in a home now she's well enough, the Comforter Wing is going to be busy this next few weeks and....oh, I've said too much...."

"Take a look at a few more homes Stan...punch in Belfast 234 on the keyboard that's my house..."

Stanley did just that and in to focus came a garden and he saw Mitch, Paddy's older brother for the first time. He was walking around the garden bumping in to things and muttering to himself under his breath.

"He always does that!" said Paddy raising his eyebrows.

He punched in few more numbers to the telescope to see some of his friends' houses.

Essex 112 showed King Bailey's small garden and Stanley was surprised how tiny it was for a King but then, he supposed, the fairies said nothing about the King or Queen of Tzus having to be rich, just wise. He was taken aback to see an enormous black and white fluffy cat in his garden, sniffing around the King's fairy door. He gasped – it must have jumped in from next door – the cheek of it!

Paris 774 for Franc and Centime's beautiful chateau, Paris 882 for Peekaboo's fancy split level apartment and balcony and then, through the very same telescope Scotland 748 for his own garden where he could see Mama filling up the bird feeders again - he found it astonishing!

"Can I see Coffee's and Phoebe's?" he enquired.

"Course you can, Coffee's is through the north telescope over there". Stan jumped down to cross the floor.

But, on the way, something caught his eye. Alongside the big and impressive telescopes in each of the four corners he saw a big black telescope in its own window with "**SPECIAL OPS ONLY**" written above it.

"What's this Pads?" he asked as he ventured towards it speedily, sensing he probably wasn't actually allowed to look through it.

Paddy jumped up from his laid back position on the swinging chair....

"No, Stan, no not that one...noooooooooooo..."

But it was too late; Stan had already hopped up the few little steps and was looking through the big telescope.

It all rather happened in slow motion as Paddy tried to get the telescope out of Stanley's paws. He had already seen what the scope was looking at and what Paddy didn't want him to see — something so ghastly and unexpected that he could barely take it in.

He looked at Paddy, woofless and ashen-faced with terror. All the happy thoughts in his head had disappeared whilst he took in everything he had just seen.

Paddy shook his head and held out his paws.

"Ok, Stanley, come on down and have a hug. I will explain what it is and about the big mission that's going to put an end to it."

Chapter 44

PUPPY Farms Stanley, Puppy Farms. The places of your worst nightmares and what you have just seen through the Special Ops telescope is one of the worst we tzus have ever known.

We rescued young Maisie from a lady who wanted her to do nothing but have puppies until she died, alone and never having known love. I have still got my eye on that one, believe me, but these people are much worse. They have been doing it for years.

There are three pairs of mummy and daddy shih tzus in there and twelve babies. They are all ill, they have never had a cuddle and I don't suppose they have ever seen daylight. They'll be sold, all those little babies, to make them people rich and I have no doubt they will be ill and wonky too. Some of them might not even make it past puppyhood, like Mabel and Myrtle's little sister. And then, those mums and dads have to make more before, one day, they will throw them out and leave them to fend for themselves in a world in which they can't even hope to survive. That's what happened to Bailey, thrown out on the streets he was, before Coffee and Nancy saw him and King Pierre sent a rescue team, it's why he is such a wise tzu.

It makes me so angry Stanley it really does — there are so many pups and dogs out there that need rescuing too and these people don't see tzus — or any dog — as a part of the family, just something to make money from.

It's outrageous.

King Leo made a promise to the fairies all those years ago that Tzu Kingdom would be a force for good and, in recent years at least, this is what we have striven to do — wipe out puppy farming and make sure that tzus only come in to a world of friendship, love and hope.

Stanley, what you have seen through that telescope is the site of one of the biggest and dangerous rescues we have ever attempted. Tanner and Phoebe have been planning it for weeks and the most senior tzus are part of the rescue team. Coffee and I will be here on Tower duty and Bonz is going to go with them as the Scout Rescue Lead.

Tanner is going to rescue the twelve babies with some very experienced rescuers — Zero, Alice, Pom Pom and Winston — and Phoebe is going to lead the six parents to safety with Kiki, Lola and Biddy with Oliver holding the fairy door open.

It's all planned and just at the final logistics stage waiting for our King Bailey and Queen Coffee to sign off the plans.

Stanley gulped and shook his head slowly.

"When are they going to be rescued Pads?"

Paddy looked at him with a serious face.

"Tomorrow."

Chapter 45

NANCY was having a stroll in the garden with Fleur when she saw Maisie appear out of the fairy door. She couldn't believe her eyes and ran over to her barking excitedly! Fleur ran over too, excited to see another Tzu in her garden.

Maisie did an enormous burp that made Fleur jump in surprise and then, she shook herself fluffy.

"Say something my sweet little Maisie...let's see if Fleur can hear you."

"Erm, I'm...."

"You're Maisie," said Fleur, "Nancy told me about you when she first arrived and was enchanted. I can hear you for a bit when you land in my garden...it's brilliant!"

Maisie was still a bit shy of people and so she ran over to Nancy.

"Oh Nancy I have missed you! I have had 'miss you pains' all over since you left." She wiped away a tear from her eye as Nancy cuddled her. "I'm bored without you and Stanley's away too."

"Well, why don't you just come and live with us here?" said Fleur. "Mummy said we would get another dog to keep Nancy company and why shouldn't that be you? I've got a princess room and we can get a dog sized bed..."

Maisie's eyes lit up. "Nancy, can I come and live here, please?"

Nancy thought for a moment and concluded that this would be just perfect. She could keep an eye on young Maisie, sharing meal times with her and make sure she was growing in to a fine young lady tzu. The youngster could play with Fleur and Skye for a lot longer after school than Nancy could these days, leaving her to snooze on Ifan's lap more. At night, she could retire to the newly built luxury Grandpops Annexe and little one could venture up the big staircase to Fleur's princess room and sleep in a velvet basket by the side of her bed.

It seemed more than perfect.

"We have to clear it with Queen Coffee and King Bailey of course Maisie but...YES!"

"She said yes" squealed Maisie and danced in circles with Fleur.

Sometimes, the solutions to problems were there, right in your head and, once you said them out loud, they just made sense.

Chapter 46

NANCY and Maisie landed in the Welcome Room and were just saying pardon as Coffee scurried past them to the café with a bundle of papers in her paws. Bailey followed with his serious face on and a large leather journal tucked under his arm.

"Miss Coffee!" said Nancy in a sing-song voice.

Coffee turned around and smiled when she saw her closest friend waving at her and stopped, whilst Bailey went ahead to the café.

"Nancy Noodle, so glad you could come back so soon and looking so beautiful. Darling friend, Bailey and I have an important meeting just about now, with Tanner and Phoebe, can I catch you later?"

"Well, I just had the most marvellous idea...well Fleur did....well..."

Nancy stopped, Coffee looked worried and every line in her fur showed. There was something big happening, she just knew it.

"What's going on?" she demanded to know.

"Nothing," answered Coffee, "it's all fine."

Nancy was far from convinced, she knew that sometimes, a leader had to get on and do things, without interference from others. Plus, she knew if Phoebe and Tanner were involved too, they could all be trusted.

"If you're sure, the thing is we wondered how you would feel about Maisie coming to live with me, Ifan, Megan, Skye and my lovely Fleur."

Coffee smiled. "It's a most excellent idea, Bailey and I were talking about it with Paddy just the other day. It should happen, as soon as possible. Look, erm, you sort it out, Mabel and Myrtle will help and I will check on you in a few days. Love you both, must dash..."

That wasn't quite the reaction either of them were hoping for and they felt a little bit flat. However, they had what they wanted — a royal stamp of approval.

At that moment, they heard two familiar voices from the West Scout Tower and Paddy jumped down followed, to Maisie's surprise, by Stan. They also looked very serious.

Stan's face lit up when he saw Maisie and they ran over to them. Everyone hugged.

"Why do you all look so cross?" said Maisie.

Paddy sighed and started to explain. "We're not cross, it's just a top secret thing that we know...."

"There's going to be a big rescue tomorrow night and there's loads of tzus involved and it's the biggest most dangerous rescue we have ever done, there's eighteen tzus from a puppy farm to save and...ooops... Pads, was I supposed to keep it a secret?"

Paddy sighed and put his head in his paws. Subtlety was not Stan's strength.

"Is that why Coffee and Bailey were meeting Phoebe and Tanner?" asked Nancy.

"It was Nance, yes it was...gather round and I will tell you all about it."

Nancy shook her head.

"You three go and have a chat — Fleur is waiting for me on the other side and I must return. But boys, we have good news. Queen Coffee has agreed that

Maisie can come and live with me, Ifan, Megan, Fleur and Skye and sleep in a princess room! I can't wait! Fleur said the best thing to do was to turn up after school and we would 'find' Maisie in the garden. Her mummy will know what to do but, she'll adopt her in the end once she sees how well we get on. So, I will leave you three to sort it out with Mabel and Myrtle and see you tonight, with Maisie about 4pm, Wales time?

"Stan, Maisie said she would like a little time with you before she comes through today — is that OK?"

He blushed and nodded. Nancy blew them all a kiss goodbye.

"I'm coming through for the party next week and I shall bring Maisie too, don't worry, I am sure everything will go well with the rescue. The tzu rescues always come good in the end — trust me."

With that she waved, laughed, blew them kisses and jumped back through her fairy door into her garden where she knew Fleur was waiting.

Chapter 47

A waiter from the café scuttled over to the sofa where Paddy, Stanley and Maisie had made themselves comfortable.

"Juice and water for everyone? Biscuits? Sausages?" he asked and then leaned in close to them and whispered, "it's getting all very serious over there, our King and Queen are just about to sign the rescue plan..."

"Does everyone know?" asked Paddy. He thought it had been a closely guarded secret known only to senior tzus and their confidantes but, judging by the whispering in the café and the amount of tzus rubber necking the meeting that was going on, he guessed that it was no more a secret than the existence of Tzu Kingdom itself!

In the knowledge that everyone knew about the rescue, Paddy decided that he would give the most intricate details to his young friends.

He explained how he would be the lead Scout in the tower, with Queen Coffee overseeing and that Bonnie would be on the ground, ensuring the rescue team could recover all 18 tzus — six parents and twelve puppies.

The rescue would commence at feeding time when the sheds in which they were living were unlocked. Tanner and Phoebe would lead the teams from the fairy door to the ramshackle sheds and throw open the cage doors. Phoebe's team would grab the three pairs of parent tzus and lead them by the paws to safety as fast as they could run — remembering that they would be weak, hungry and unaccustomed to light and that some of them would need carrying. Because of the locked door, the scouts hadn't been able to do a full assessment meaning they would have to hope there was enough tzu-power to carry out the rescue.

Meanwhile, Tanner, the most experienced rescuer of all, and his team would grab three baby tzus each and once they were sure they had all twelve they would sprint back through to Tzu Kingdom and down to the Comforter Wing. Oliver would hold back by the fairy door to ensure they could all jump through when they arrived back at the tree.

"Oh...that's why there's extra beds being made up by the Comforter Tzus, it all makes sense now. No wonder everyone is keen for me to head off to my new life as Fleur's dog! Wow! I am so impressed by the amount of planning that you do!" said Maisie.

Stan jumped up, full of courage and determination.

"I want to go on the rescue — if I was brave enough to rescue Maisie then I am brave enough to help Phoebe and Tanner tomorrow."

"Not this one Stan," said Paddy touching his friend's shoulder "this is a very big deal. It's just too risky before you have had your training. You can sit in Scout Tower with Coffee and me if you want to."

"No, I am going to talk to the King and Queen," and with that, he marched through the café to interrupt the meeting with his offer, muttering "brave as a lion" to himself underneath his furrowed brow.

Chapter 48

BAILEY took the pen from Coffee to add the final seal to the plans for the rescue.

"You've done an excellent job, both of you," he said to Phoebe and Tanner, "and we are both extremely proud."

He looked down to the leather book to see a furry paw covering the signature area. At the end of it was a cross-faced Stanley. Maisie and Paddy ran in to the café after him.

"Let me help on this rescue please King Bailey".

"No, not this time young man, certainly not."

"Oh please please please....because..."

"Stanley," said Queen Coffee, sternly, stomping her front paw on the table, "please DO NOT disobey the Tzu King."

Stanley was shocked to hear Coffee talk so sharply but knew he deserved it. He went to answer back and then remembered, Bailey and Coffee were King and Queen because they were the wisest of them all and decided not to argue with them, especially since he had learnt his lesson the last time he had doubted their intentions.

"Sorry." he said.

Bailey's face softened. He stroked Stanley's head and spoke kindly.

"Stanley, you are as brave as a lion, we all know that, but this is the biggest rescue we have ever attempted. Tanner and Phoebe have worked hard organising this with highly trained rescuers and scouts – this is not an adventure for newbies."

Stan wiped his paw across his eyes, trying not to show how upset he was. "Sorry King Bailey, sorry Queen Coffee."

Coffee spoke and broke the awkward silence.

"Look, here's an idea, my darling, why doesn't Stanley come and observe in Scout Tower with Paddy and me? I suppose we could do with a runner to assist and he will PROMISE not to do anything rash...won't he?"

He nodded. He was a good boy, just a little impetuous at times.

"Ahem" came a very small voice "perhaps I could observe too and make the tea and keep Stan under control? I could bring some snacks?" enquired Maisie.

Paddy's ears pricked up at the mention of snacks and everyone giggled, breaking a very tense moment. Coffee and Bailey looked at each other, then at Phoebe, Tanner and Paddy. They all nodded.

"Oh go on then!" said King Bailey, laughing raucously, with a twinkle in his eye.

He amended the book to include Stanley and Maisie as 'Scout Tower Assistants' before putting his official signature on the page, next to Coffee's.

The rescue was going ahead, with a little Stan and Maisie shaped amendment to the plan.

Chapter 49

STANLEY and Maisie had a little time to spend together in the Comforter Wing before she was to go to her new home later this afternoon.

She was pleased to get back and see the dandelion clocks by her bed. She asked Stan if it would be alright to present them to Mabel and Myrtle to say thank you for making her better. Stan was only too pleased to agree to this and they tied them up with a lilac bow and wrote a thank you note, knowing they would find them when they came into the room later.

They set about helping to get the rooms ready for the arrival of all the dogs and puppies that who would be seeking refuge after escaping their puppy farming ordeal. They made up beds in both rooms, opened the windows for fresh air, folded up clean pyjamas for the puppies, lined up toothpaste and shampoo in the bathrooms, tided up any bowls in to the kitchen, swept the floors and, finally, placed Millicent on the big bed to watch over everyone in the Girls' Room. This had been Maisie's home for many weeks and now it was time for her to be brave and pass it over to those who needed it more. She was not going to be able to take Millicent to her home straight away because, well, 'lost dogs' just don't turn up in people's gardens with their own teddy bear so she had bravely volunteered to leave Millicent behind on the understanding that she would take her one day soon but, for now, her clean, pink teddy that had seen her through such a lot would remain to give comfort to other rescued tzus.

Stanley was immensely proud. It was rescuing Millicent for Maisie that had nearly led to dire consequences back in that horrible garden when that was all Maisie had in the world. She had a lot more of late and she was a brave, grown up tzu going to a new home and making her own way in the world. 'That dark and scary night seemed like a lifetime ago,' he thought as he looked at her plumping up cushions for the new intake.

Plus, she had Nancy and Fleur waiting on the other side to give her a home. She was the luckiest tzu and now, it was time for others to benefit from the cuddles of Millicent and the kindness of the sisters, Franc and Centime.

Chapter 50

THERE was one very important thing that Maisie had to do before she went to her new home and, having sought the approval of Nancy, she led Stanley down the winding corridors, through the Welcome Room and to the very back of the Party Room where a pair of black curtains hung.

"You ready boyfriend?" she said to a curious faced Stanley and reached up with her key in her paw to unlock the door. She flung the door open with a big "TA DA"!

"Oh my," said Stan, "what is this place?"

"It's 'Tzu Gallery' my Stanley. It used to be a very big part of Tzu Kingdom but King Bailey shut it up some years ago and wouldn't let anyone in. I had to find the key from where it was hidden."

"It displays all the portraits of all the Kings and Queens of Tzu Kingdom and it has paintings of some of the historic moments too."

"Stan, Bailey shut it up because he doesn't think his painting is worthy of hanging here with all the others like King Leo, Queen Mirabelle or King Hamish. But he is the only person who feels like this and we have to make this right — for him and for Coffee because they are both worthy of celebrating. She doesn't let it show but it does upset her because she is proud of her days as a scout and her wonderful husband, but Bailey won't hear of it. He doesn't know he is upsetting her because she hides it from him — literally

— did you know she keeps their only wedding photo in her pocket? This should be on the wall as well."

Stanley was admiring the Kings and Queens and some of the paintings of amazing things that had happened and were depicted on the opposite wall — the colourful painting of the tzus freeing the fairies, the return of the team who staged the first puppy farm rescue, the signing of the Peace Treaty masterminded by King Wolfgang during the human war and the unveiling of Scout Tower by King Nemo.

"Well, of course it should. Maisie, how can we put this right? I am not an artist and you is going to have to settle in to your new home and well, there's the rescue ..."

"Stan. I have a plan."

Maisie updated him on her meeting earlier in the week with Colin. Stan had quite forgotten that Colin had taken up art since he was unable to be a rescuer and started working in the Welcome Room.

"Maisie, I remember what Colin told me that night we rescued you — he likes arts and crafts and especially painting more than he liked being a rescuer. He thinks that is his calling."

"I know Stan, we discussed this too so it must be true, but Bailey just won't believe him. He just carries on thinking he ruined Colin's life and blaming himself, upsetting Coffee at the same time just because he won't talk about it with anyone."

"What can we do to mend all this, Maisie Moppet?"

Maisie explained her plan.

The first stage was to dust, clean and straighten what was there in the Gallery, and to see if anyone was missing from the Kings and Queens wall.

The second stage was for Colin to start painting any missing Kings and Queens which would, no doubt, include Bailey and Coffee's Royal portrait. He'd already started some sketches and Nancy had given her the Royal lineage for Colin to work on so they could re-establish the Royal Wall. The young tzus would be able to educate themselves on each Royal leader, what they did whilst they were ruling and how long they reigned for.

Stage Three would be to use the Scout Paperwork to ensure that there was a picture of each tzu currently enjoying Tzu Kingdom on the "Tzu Family" wall.

Stage Four would be a sad one, because this would be to make the 'Remember Wall' where tzus who had fallen asleep for the last time would be remembered. It was sad to think that every tzu would move from the Family to Remember Wall at some time but this way, they would all be remembered with happiness and no one would never forget them.

Stage Five would be to make a wall for photos and paintings of key moments in Tzu History and it would be for more than just big occasions like the story of King Leo, it would be interspersed with photos of parties and fun times and be called the 'Moments Wall'.

"You have put a lot of thought in to this Maisie" said Stanley, looking worried. "Who is going to do all this?"

"Ahem."

"Colin!" they both shouted.

Chapter 51

COLIN and Maisie's meeting back in the Comforter Wing set the "Tzu Gallery Project" — TGP — in motion and he was tremendously excited to be at the heart of it.

No matter how many times he had tried to tell Bailey he was happy that his career had changed direction it fell on deaf ears. The King was absorbed by his grief over Colin's injuries - something big was going to have to happen before he took notice. Colin had experience of changing careers with his two dads. His Dadsy had been on the stage in London and New York all the time before Colin came along but a few years of ill health had seen an end to his and now he had a new job on the television, judging other people -what Pops laughingly called "scoring their Macbeths". He wasn't quite sure what that was, but what he did know was that it meant that they were able to get a dog and Colin was delighted that was him they rescued from Battersea Dogs Home. Pops made musicals happen (that's how they met) and he travelled all over Europe — sometimes taking Dadsy and Colin with him too. Colin had a pet passport and he stayed in some of the best hotels in the world.

The night that Maisie came looking for the key was one of the happiest since he had been part of Tzu Kingdom — and certainly since the incident.

Together, they hatched the plan that had just been explained to Stanley.

They wanted to re-launch Tzu Gallery at the next party so there was no time to do everything before then.

The "Remember Wall" was very important with all the dearly departed tzus to add yet they hadn't got a hope of remembering everyone, so they felt they should involve the elder tzus in this part of the TGP and Colin, and any other artistic tzu, could paint from their memories. For now, it would remain empty until they felt sure they could make an extremely good job of it.

"I love all these plans, they are so sensible," said Stanley, "and I would love to help you and Colin whilst you are settling in."

"That would be great Stan, Maisie will need to settle a bit first but she has worked out all what we need to do. So, I am going to get to work today straightening everything up and seeing if anything needs repairing from the oldest paintings. Then, I shall work more on my Bailey and Coffee painting — look here's my sketches."

Colin unfurled a roll of paper from under his smock and they gasped as they saw the most beautiful picture of the Royal couple, paw in paw, sat in their thrones, looking at each other lovingly. They weren't a couple for pomp and circumstance and, although they were wearing their formal cloaks and crowns in the picture, they were relaxed and happy looking.

"You've captured them just right Colin, our beautiful King and Queen. Who are the other sketches of?" Stanley asked.

"It's going to be a big project so I have started on just a few of our special friends to start with and I have put them in groups mainly in places where we think of them...such as...Paddy and Phoebe canoodling in Scout Tower..."

"Is that why they are always up there?" said Stan.

Colin coughed and then continued without comment.

"Here's a nice one of Mabel and Myrtle in the Comforter Wing, Kiki and Lola doing each other's fur, Tanner looking brave going on a rescue, Pom Pom and Alice doing a fitness trail and...oh this is a nice one, look...here's a picture of Franc and Centime with Peekaboo in Paris..."

Maisie almost fainted at the beautiful picture of the glamourous French trio in the shadow of the Eiffel Tower with their long flowing locks and amazing Parisian style."

"Oh Colin," she said pawing Centime's ear on the painting and admiring Peekaboo's skater dress, "when you paint me, please...will you paint me like one of your French Tzus?"

Colin promised he would and somehow, Stan knew that he was destined to be painted wearing a beret.

Chapter 52

MAISIE locked up Tzu Gallery and popped the key back in the drawer where she found it. Colin said he would keep it safe and that there was no way King Bailey would come looking for it whilst this big rescue was planned, meaning it was safe in the Welcome Room. She put it back in a lower drawer so that she could reach it quickly and easily. It seemed funny now that she had secretly tried to find it when she could have just asked Colin.

The boys both had to go home for the day after they discussed TGP. Colin went first so that Maisie and Stan could have some time together. He had to get back to Mama for tea and also because their favourite comedy programme was on at home. He needed to be there to chortle with her on the sofa and then cuddle with Daddy when he arrived back from work.

He walked Maisie back to the Comforter Wing to get Mabel and Myrtle because they were going to pass her over to Nancy at 4pm through, what would become, her very own shared fairy door. It was a big moment but Maisie didn't want any fuss.

"I think there was enough fuss when I arrived," she twinkled to Stan as they walked down the corridor, "and I will be back tomorrow to help you in Scout Tower of course."

"I know but I won't be sure to see you every time I come through now," he answered, despondently.

They hugged each other. Their bond was strong as it

could be, yet it would be a little bit different now.

"Stan, it doesn't stop Coffee and Bailey from being a married pair of tzus or Paddy and Phoebe from canoodling, so it will all be fine, I promise."

Smiling, they arrived back at the Comforter Wing. It looked the same although it felt a bit different with eighteen beds, six adult and twelve puppy size, all made up for the rescue aftermath. The sisters said they would let the rescued sleep in family groups and they would move the beds around when they arrived rather than have boys and girls rooms for this big rescue.

Millicent the teddy bear was sat on top of the four poster bed that Maisie got better in. She looked down from her cushion as her owner jumped up on the bed and gave her one last cuddle.

"You've got a very important task ahead of you young lady," she said, "make sure you do your job well, make these tzus better, I'll be back to help as often as I can." She kissed her and nuzzled in to her fur.

"Brave as a lion cub," she said as she jumped down.

The four of them walked down the long corridor to the Welcome Room where Lennon was on duty. The sisters blushed, they both thought he was so handsome.

Stan kissed Maisie goodbye. "I love you," he said, "Love you too," said Maisie.

"OK, sweetie, let's jump through and in to Nancy's paws. Mabel will stay here with Stan and then we will get him home too" said Myrtle.

They barked loud and firm and jumped. They were gone.

Stan squeezed Mabel's paw tight. He looked around and sighed.

'Brave as a lion,' he mumbled.

Chapter 53

BACK at home on the sofa with Mama, Stan was in a funny mood. Myrtle had come back through the fairy door smiling from ear to ear and saying how lovely Fleur was, something Stanley knew anyway after he had met her with Paddy that day, and telling him how perfect her family and her house were for a small girl tzu. Fleur had brought little Skye with her to meet Maisie and they had skipped off as a vision in pink so he knew the right home had been found for his girlfriend. He knew he would see her loads when he went to Tzu Kingdom, they were on Scout Tower Assistant duty tomorrow even, nevertheless he was a little anxious about that too with a lot of his friends on such a dangerous mission.

As Nancy had said, rescues always worked out in the end, but it was a big deal and clearly causing Coffee and Bailey to be worried.

The whole puppy farm thing was worrying him too. He just couldn't get over how lucky he was. He still saw his tzu birth-mum every now again, and one of his brothers, Jake. They were born in a nice warm house and snuggled on blankets together whilst they were little puppies. Then Mama and Daddy had come to get him one Friday afternoon and he started to build his life with them, as a family. He was their first ever dog and he would stay with them forever and ever too.

He sighed again and then felt Mama's arms around him.

"You **OK** poppet? Do you fancy a little walk before our programme starts? We could just go round the block, blow those cobwebs away?"

'Do you know what **Mama**?' thought **Stanley**. 'I think you are right. Let's have some 'mother and son' time and just do some dog stuff. Maybe we could throw a ball?'

'Tomorrow's a big day, but that doesn't mean we can't enjoy today.'

He jumped off the sofa and ran to the front door, excitedly barking and dancing!

She put on his lead as he picked up his favourite throwy ball and off they both went, seemingly, without a care in the world.

Chapter 54

EVERYTHING was in place the next day. Queen Coffee, Paddy, Maisie and Stanley were in Scout Tower keeping an eye on the puppy farm from where they would rescue eighteen shih tzus. All young or puppies, all poorly and all unloved. Tzu Kingdom was about to put a stop to that.

At the fairy door wall, King Bailey was in final conversation with Tanner, Phoebe and Bonnie. All the rescuers were lined up, wearing their camouflage jackets, rescuer badges and caps. There was a lot of excitement and tzus were buzzing around the café and the bar, both open for drinks. Franc and Centime were on duty for the Comforter Wing with Peekaboo drafted in to help them take the rescued down to the freshly made beds. Hopefully, there would be no injuries amongst the rescue team for them to worry about, but there were a few more tzus on standby, just in case.

He cleared his throat and tapped his paw on the Welcome Room desk. Carmen put down her knitting and opened the phone line to Scout Tower for the King's speech.

"Tzus...friends...this is a big night in Tzu Kingdom and it has all been carefully planned. Our two lead rescuers and I have assembled an awesome team to get these poor friends-we-are-yet-to-know to safety and our Queen Coffee has put together an equally awesome back up scout, medical, communications and welcome team to complement it.

"Tonight, the weather in the human world is worse than we expected. It is stormy and gloomy but the rescue team want to go ahead because the scout team have advised that this rescue can wait no longer — those poor dogs are at risk from some terrible humans."

"If we stick to the plan, we can have everyone back to safety in no time at all, but we absolutely **must** stick to the plan."

"Remember, Queen Coffee and I love you all."

"Be careful. Be brave. Be Tzu."

An enormous cheer went up as Tanner and Phoebe hugged the King and the entire rescue team jumped through the fairy doors one by one.

Coffee and Paddy were on the West and Special Ops telescopes, and the whole Kingdom held its breath as everyone waited to hear news from Paddy and Coffee via the Scout Tower loud speaker system.

"OK, they're through and advancing" bellowed Paddy's voice into the Welcome Room. The noise got louder in the communal areas as they excitedly discussed the latest.

King Bailey paced up and down, down and up and around and around.

A few minutes later, Paddy's voice again.

"The sheds are unlocked as we thought they would be...they're in. Oliver is on guard by the fairy door and Bonz is with him."

"Alice and Pom Pom are back in view...they've got three babies each REPEAT three babies each. They are running back to the fairy door...Oliver is shouting it open...they're coming through.."

Everyone gasped and waited and then BUMP BURP BURP BURP as the two tzus came through, their paws full of hiccupping puppies.

"Six down, twelve to go" said Alice.

"We'll run them straight down to the Comforter Room, their parents are coming next..." said Pom Pom as they started to run.

Coffee's voice bellowed out to the crowd...

"Attention everyone, Biddy is on his way back with two adult tzus...father tzu carrying mother...Biddy holding his paw and leading him to the door...Oliver barking..."

The fairy door opened again and various gaseous noises rung out.

"She's not very well," said Biddy "he's ok but he's skinny. I'll take them down with Centime for some nursing."

Off went Biddy and Centime and another landing caught them by surprise as Winston landed back with three more babies in his arms.

"Winston's back everyone," shouted Paddy, "that's nine puppies, three to go and two parents, four to go. We've not been seen by the wicked people let's GO GO GO."

Up in Scout Tower, Stanley and Maisie were having the time of their lives watching all the action as it happened! They jumped up and high pawed each other every time somefur came back and had even forgotten about the snacks and drinks that were there for the scouts — it was just too exciting.

"Nancy was right," said Stanley, "rescues do all work out fine! We need not have worried so much!"

"I know," said Maisie "this is honestly the most exciting thing ever — even more exciting than my own rescue!"

"Zero's got three more, that's the last of the puppies," shouted Paddy and the cheer went up from down below as Zero brought the final puppies through.

"Zero you're a hero," said King Bailey as he landed just a few minutes after Winston, "how are they faring?"

"It's horrible down there my King, horrible, and the weather is dreadful so we can hardly hear each other, but if we get them looked after I think they'll all be OK given time. The mothers are in a terrible state, they truly need our help and maybe good human help soon as poss..."

"OK Zero, we will sort it out in the morning my brave rescuer. Take the little ones down with Franc and we will start getting them better."

Then everyone heard Coffee's voice again.

"Kiki and Lola are coming back, but they've only got three tzus between them...what's happened to the other one...oh hang on, there's Tanner now, carrying her.

Kiki and Lola jumped through with two father tzus and a weak and exhausted mother, bravely running, knowing her babies were on the other side.

"We will go straight down with them," they said and ran off, with Peekaboo in hot pursuit.

Paddy was back on the loudspeaker.

"Tanner's coming back with Phoebe and the final mother tzu. I can hardly see, the rain is lashing down and there's thunder too...he's shouting to Oliver and Bonz to jump through now and they'll follow. Quick guys, I can see a nasty man coming in to view now — oh no he's seen them!"

King Bailey was biting his claws and trying to be calm and then breathed a sigh of relief as Oliver, Bonnie and then Tanner jumped through with the final rescued tzu. He waited for Phoebe to appear.

Phoebe didn't follow. Bailey looked at Tanner.

"MAY DAY MAY DAY." shouted Coffee from Scout Tower.

Stan and Maisie rose to their feet and ran over to a woofless Paddy, still clinging to the telescope with his head lowered.

"Feebs....my Feebs...no...no..." he cried.

172

Chapter 55

FROM noisy and excited at the return of the final rescue party, suddenly things went very quiet when Phoebe failed to appear through the fairy door. There was cheering and clapping when Tanner landed but it died down as the seconds ticked by and she wasn't there behind him.

Bonnie was perceptive and she took the mother tzu from Tanner and gently carried her down to the Comforter Room.

"She was right behind me, right behind me," Tanner kept saying. Bailey put his paw on his shoulder and stared again at the fairy door.

"Any second now, she'll be back," he said, hopefully.

Queen Coffee jumped down from the North rope stair ladder to Scout Tower, followed by Stanley and Maisie.

"She went back, we don't know why?" she explained. "Tanner, what happened?"

"I have no idea Queen Coffee, no idea. We had every last one, I told Oliver to jump through with Bonnie and we would follow so I knew everyone would be safe and then, well, she must have gone back for something or, more likely, *somefur*."

"You mean Phoebe, of all tzus, went off the plan?" said Stanley, remembering that he had been quite severely reprimanded by her for this. "That means it must be serious."

Coffee turned to Bailey and reassured him as much as she could.

"My love, she was just about to jump through and then we saw her ears prick up and she ran back to the shed. But, she didn't come out. The nasty man saw and locked her in."

"Our Phoebe's trapped, on a puppy farm, at the mercy of the most evil humans in the world."

"Well, we need a new plan to rescue her" said Stanley.

There was a moment of complete silence and then the door to the West Rope Ladder swung open and slammed against the wall. Paddy jumped down, wearing a camouflage jacket slightly on the small side, a hat to match and a determined face.

"Right. I'm off to rescue me Feebs. Anyone with me or am I going it alone?"

Stanley and Maisie looked at each other.

"WE ARE!" they shouted, grabbing camouflage jackets of their own that had been discarded by other rescuers.

"Come on then" he said.

"Two seconds," said Maisie and jumped over the Welcome Room desk and grabbed something out of a drawer, tucking it in her pocket.

She grabbed Stanley's paw.

"Ready now?" Paddy glared.

She nodded and the three of them barked loudly and firmly and jumped through the fairy door to rescue Phoebe.

Chapter 56

PHOEBE knew she had heard another voice in the shed, her hearing was exceptionally good and had never failed her. Just as Tanner was about to jump through she heard the poorly mother tzu through the wind and the rain ask if they had Molly and little Beth. She quickly worked out that this was a mother and daughter and certainly not any of those they had already rescued because there had been at least two in each litter.

As soon as she got back to the shed she heard the door slam behind her and the nasty man locked it. Well, she thought, I can't do anything about that so I will just hope and trust in my rescuer team to help me. She knew she had gone off plan, she consoled herself with the knowledge that, just like Stanley before her, she had probably done the right thing.

She heard sobbing and followed it to the most horrible space she had ever seen in her tzu life. Tiny, stinky and filthy it housed just one very small and desperately weak mother tzu and in her paws was the tinniest puppy she had ever laid eyes on.

"Hello, I'm Phoebe," she whispered, and the little tzu looked up.

"I'm Molly and this is Beth, she's not well, I am not sure she will make it through the night and, if she doesn't the man will put an end to me too...I'm just not useful any more, he says."

"You will both be fine, I'm sure of it," said Phoebe, not even in the slightest bit sure.

She took her jacket off and wrapped it around them, then put her paws around both, sitting quietly trapped together. For how long she just didn't know. She sung sweetly to them and rocked them backwards and forwards.

Chapter 57

PADDY, Stanley and Maisie arrived in the horrible place in need of a plan. Luckily, Maisie had started to sketch one out in her head. It was the reason that she had stopped off at the Welcome Room desk.

"OK, right, I'm going in." said Paddy.

"How you going to get through the door? It's locked." said Stan.

"Not sure, but my Feebs is in there so I will find a way," he replied. He was being ever so stroppy, of course Stan knew he was worried beyond worried — he hadn't mentioned food for ages — but someone had to be sensible.

"But you can't do that Paddy, you could get trapped too and what would Mitch do without you in his old age? And what about your mam?"

Paddy sat down on the floor with his head in his paws. He felt like Phoebe was lost forever to him and all those that loved her and, the truth was, he had no idea what to do.

"You need an enchanted key I think," said Maisie, and proudly produced a key from her pocket.

"But, how do you know it's enchanted?" said Stanley, whilst Paddy looked on hopefully.

"I don't, but it might be, and I don't think there's another plan is there?"

There most certainly was not.

"It's worth a try Stanley." said Paddy, hoping it would work.

The three friends quickly weighed up all the pros and cons, deciding that the safest thing would be to send the two boys to rescue Phoebe, in case there was someone to carry. Maisie was stronger, but not quite strong enough to carry anyone or to run as fast as she needed to and, besides, someone needed to bark open the fairy door. She entrusted Stanley with the key and watched nervously.

The boys ran to the shed and stood by the locked door.

"Feebs," said Paddy "you in there?"

"Paddy...I am so glad to hear your voice, can you get in and rescue us, I have two others in need of rescue with me that we never saw. It's not your fault because they were locked here at the back of the shed — there's no way you or any of the scouts could have seen them."

He felt bad about missing them and hoped he could rescue them all, but he knew couldn't reach the lock and he looked at his friend for help. Stanley understood and jumped on his shoulders where he put the key in and tried to turn it. It wouldn't budge. It looked like it wasn't enchanted after all and now he had no idea if they could rescue Phoebe or even get back themselves.

It looked like the six of them had landed in mortal peril. Worse still, they couldn't be seen from Scout Tower here.

Back at the fairy door, Maisie was keeping a careful watch on events and saw the disappointment in the boys' faces when the key wouldn't work. She must have been wrong, she felt so sure the key was magic and then, she felt a flutter and a spark behind her ear. She spun round and there was a fairy, flying right next to her and she couldn't believe her eyes.

The fairy giggled and winked. Maisie knew what she had to do.

"Try the lock again Stan," she shouted, "quickly, the nasty man is coming out of the house...quickly!" she screamed.

The key tingled in Stanley's paw and he knew something was different about it. He looked again at his surroundings and knew he couldn't leave Phoebe here. He turned it in the lock and it moved with ease and the door flung open.

"We're in!" he said and jumped down off Paddy's shoulders and they ran in to see Phoebe with two tiny tzus, one just a puppy.

"Paddy, oh my Paddy this is Molly and Beth, they are so ill."

He kissed her and patted tiny Beth. "Feebs. We got to run my lovely."

Paddy picked them both up and Stanley hoisted Phoebe to her paws.

"We need to get through the fairy door like NOW!" said Stanley, seriously and panicked.

"RRRUUUUNNNN" he shouted, just like when they were rescuing Maisie.

Phoebe and the boys ran as fast as they could, Paddy carrying Molly and Beth, to where they had come in, grabbed Maisie's paw, barked loudly and firmly and everyone jumped right back to safety.

Chapter 58

QUEEN Coffee was the first to see the group of six jump through the fairy door and she gasped, first with the welcome sight of her close friend Phoebe, then at those youngsters who had mounted such a brave and impromptu rescue of her and, finally, at the terrible state of the young mother and pup with them.

She was there in a flash, with King Bailey and Tanner in hot pursuit.

"Children, oh my children, are you all OK? Phoebe are you hurt?"

"I'm fine Coffee, we all are, but there were two more to rescue — I only heard them as I got to the fairy door the first time. No one could have seen them, they were hidden away at the back of the shed."

Coffee felt terrible, as Chief Scout she had missed these two and they were the ones who most needed rescuing, for sure.

"Coffee. Phoebe. I need your help. She's fading." said Paddy, quietly.

The ladies ran over to Paddy as he laid Molly and Beth down on a pile of bean bags.

"Molly," said Phoebe, "you are going to be fine, we are going to look after you and make you both well."

Slowly, she shook her head and reached out to her new friend.

"It's too late for me wonderful, kind Phoebe, it just hurts all too much. Thank you, thank you for rescuing me and showing me love and kindness but, I can't fight any more. I have just one wish before I close my eyes...will you promise to look after Beth and love her for me, make sure she finds a home and that she knows love, friendship and beauty all around...and, please, tell her that her mummy loved her with all her heart."

"I promise Molly, I will love little Beth as if she is my own." said Phoebe.

Molly held Beth close, whispered "I love you my princess" kissed her daughter's nose and closed her tired eyes for the very last time.

Chapter 59

SILENCE fell over all of Tzu Kingdom, except for the weeping of the younger tzus who found this all too much. Everyone was distraught – there hadn't been a death in this happy place for years – not since the human war time when King Wolfgang had been their leader and no one could remember that far back to the point that they had even forgotten this even could happen.

Phoebe took tiny Beth from Molly's arms and held her close. She was so small and fragile.

"I'm taking Beth to the Comforter Wing," she said, fighting back the tears.

"Would you like help?" said Coffee.

"I'll be fine Coffee, thank you, it is me who made the promise to Molly and that starts right now."

She carried Beth carefully across the Welcome Room and down the corridor, holding her close and stroking her ears. She was tiny but she seemed to know what had happened and she whimpered quietly into Phoebe's fur.

King Bailey addressed everyone who remained in the room.

"Tzus, this indeed is a sad day and in time we will find a fitting tribute to poor sweet Molly. Tanner, Lennon and I will conduct a short funeral in the garden if you would all like to join us. Molly may have not known love in her world but, for the all too short time she was in ours she did and we will always consider her to be our friend. It is the love of Tzu Kingdom and our Phoebe in particular that allowed her to pass away peacefully knowing her puppy was in safe paws."

"We must not forget that we have successfully saved six adult tzus and thirteen puppies this evening and congratulate all of those involved in the rescues. We must concentrate on their full recovery and ensure they have a bright future thanks to Tzu Kingdom."

"Friends, take a drink, enjoy some comforting food, talk to each other and come to terms with what has happened. But know that we could not have done more than we did for Molly and that, as well as supporting Phoebe to keep the promise she made to Molly, we are also fulfilling the promise we made to the fairies in the days of King Leo."

The tzus mumbled their agreement in respectful silence and moved close to their friends.

"We have new friends among our number now and we must be happy that they are safe away from the evils of puppy farming. In time, we will find them superb homes and ensure they have the happy life that each one of them deserves, as we do."

"Spend some time with your human families too, because they love you and I decree that the scheduled party will go ahead as planned. We will use it to celebrate friendship and love in honour of those tzus less fortunate."

Coffee looked on proudly, thinking that he certainly knew how to say just the right thing as the tzus clapped and hugged their friends.

Chapter 60

MAISIE was exhausted from the rescue and Stanley took her straight home to where Nancy was waiting. It seemed like a long night, yet everything had happened so quickly. She was a little tearful about Molly; there was little Stan could say. He kissed her goodnight and left her to go off to bed in her pink princess room, knowing that she would be happy in her basket next to Fleur's bed.

Returning to the café, he saw that Colin had arrived and was having a drink with Paddy.

For once, Paddy was very calm and he was telling the story like it happened without his usual embellishments. He must have been feeling a little bit better though as his bacon and egg roll arrived just as he did, accompanied by a plate of sausages on the side.

"Sausage fellas? Help yourselves!" and they took one each, leaving the rest for Paddy to enjoy.

"What a night! Twenty rescued. One lost. Nineteen in recovery and Feebs has a puppy."

Colin shook his head. "There's not been a funeral actually here in our time, it's so rare. Tzus usually just come here less and less and well...you know..."

Stanley interrupted. "I loved Bailey's speech in the Welcome Room and outside at the funeral. He's a brilliant King, he was so brave to say all those things and get us to talk to each other about what happened, it means that, you know, it's out there and we can remember how Molly loved Beth and we can celebrate that and remember her for always, rather than just thinking of her as the tzu that died."

"We did the best for her Stanley — otherwise she would not have been remembered and who knows what would have become of little Beth? It got me to thinking" said Colin "I have got an idea on how we can remember Sweet Molly, but we can't tell King Bailey for now, it has to be a secret or we will blow our cover on the TGP."

"What? What's TGP?" said Paddy, in between sausages.

Stanley and Colin brought their pal up to speed on the re-launch of Tzu Gallery and the plans that Maisie had made for them.

He laughed.

"So you're doing all the work then and she's just supervising? She's sure got leadership skills that little one, she's an inspiration!"

Chapter 61

COLIN worked hard on his sketches every day in the Welcome Room and he was pleased with how they were all coming along. Together with Stanley and Paddy, he had cleaned and re-hung all the portraits and, with just a few days to go now, Tzu Gallery was looking unquestionably special again.

All the portraits of the Kings and Queens had been accounted for, right through from King Leo to King Pierre. He now just had to finish the official portrait of Bailey and Coffee, complete their wedding painting — taken from the polaroid Coffee carried in her pocket - and one other special picture that was to take pride of place on the day.

He had also sketched many of his close friends and he was proud that everyone seemed happy with his work. He had finished the painting of Paddy and Phoebe now and was just putting the final touches to the one of Maisie and Stanley. In fact, she was due for a sitting any moment now and he paced at the fairy door waiting for her to come through, paintbrush in paw.

Just as he was thinking there might have been a change of plan, Maisie landed with a bump through the fairy door and skidded across the floor.

She shook herself all over and stifled a burp in her paw.

"Hi Colin, goodness me I nearly didn't get here at all. Fleur's mummy is putting an advert in the local paper to say she has found a dog and to see if anyone is looking for me and she was trying to get a good photo to put with it. Well, we know no one is but Fleur, Nancy and me are all playing along!

"She says I can stay if nobody claims me...as if that nasty lady would want me back after Stan made her fall over!"

"Well, looks like you are well sorted there Maisie, I don't suppose you'll be claimed by nasty lady because you look nothing like how you did on the first night when we found you."

"Unrecognisable" retorted Maisie, swishing her long flowing ears.

She hopped up on a stool to allow Colin to finish his sketch. She wanted to look French in the portrait like Peekaboo and Centime and he had painted her with Stanley on the Champs-Élysées, Stan wearing a jaunty beret.

"Colin, how are all the rescued tzus now?"

It had been a few days since the big rescue and things had certainly calmed down but there was a lot of loving and nursing to do before any of them could go to new homes or be passed to Knowers.

"Well, mixed news on that front Maisie. The adult boys are generally OK, they just need a lot of soup and a bit of weight on and they'll be right as rain, I reckon they will be well enough to come and make some new friends at the party.

"Two of the mothers are confined to bed until they are a lot better, the third one is not bad considering and she's been up, chatting and stuff with Mabel and Myrtle."

"As for the puppies I don't know how all those boys and girls survived — there's six of each — and they are being cared for around the clock. They are poorly and wonky but they've drawn great strength from being out of that awful place and being in Tzu Kingdom."

"And then there's Beth."

He shook his head and put his paintbrush down. Maisie spun around.

"What?" she asked.

"I don't know Maisie, I just don't know. She's so small and weak. She's just lying there in that big bed, she's not uttering a word. She drinks a little milk but...it's not looking good. Phoebe's getting very despondent...she made a promise to young Molly but who knows if she's going to be able to keep it if, well, you know..."

Something popped into her head as if a lightbulb had gone on and she jumped down off her stool.

"I think it's time for Maisie to go and help a tzu less fortunate," she asserted, heading off to the Comforter Wing, "and I have a plan."

Chapter 62

THE delightful sound of giggling greeted Maisie as she ventured in to the Comforter Wing and there was a real sight for sore eyes. Mabel and Myrtle were in their rocking chairs with twelve baby tzus sat around them on colourful beanbags.

"You can't be 'Iron', you might as well be 'washing machine' or 'cooker hob'" she heard Mabel say, laughing, followed by the sounds of chortling puppies.

They saw Maisie and all gasped, she cut quite a dash these days and had the capacity to turn heads when she entered a room.

Myrtle came to greet her.

"Children, this is our little Maisie. She was a patient in here before you, we rescued her from a puppy farm too. We have made her all better and now she has a home with an elder tzu called Nancy and a lovely family and she sleeps in a princess bed."

She waved hello at them all, as they stared at her in awe, hoping they would look like her one day soon.

"Why were you all talking about irons?" she quizzed, making them all laugh.

"Oh, well, we have twelve tzus here needing names and, so, the girls decided they all wanted to be named after jewels so please meet Diamond, Ruby, Emerald, Sapphire, Amber and Coral," said Mabel as each of the girls waved from their beanbag as they heard their new name, wearing the pyjamas that Maisie herself had put out for them a few days earlier.

"Well, then we set about naming these boys and they decided they wanted to be named after metals so we decided on Goldie, Copper, Silver, Bronzer, Zinc and...well then we got a bit stuck and someone shouted out Iron! It made us all laugh — you can't call a dog Iron!"

"How about Cobalt?" offered Maisie.

"I like that," said Cobalt, who was quite pleased he didn't have to be called 'Iron' after all "'Cob' for short!" and the puppies began to say their own names and introduce each other, proud as punch to be called something at last.

"Could I please go and see Beth?" she asked. Mabel and Myrtle looked at each other nervously.

"Maisie, she is a very poorly little girl, are you sure you are up to seeing her? It might make you ever so upset."

"Well, I rescued her so I have seen her at her worst."

The sisters looked at each other and seemed to be communicating without saying anything. Siblings could do that sometimes, it was like they didn't need words to know what each other was thinking.

"OK Maisie, because you are a clever girl and we trust you then you can go and see her. But she isn't in a good way, she hasn't spoken since Phoebe brought her back. It's thoroughly upsetting Phoebe because she promised to take care of her and, well, it's just not looking like she is going to be able to keep the promise she made to her mother Molly," said Mabel.

"Maybe you might be able to relate to her and get her to understand what it means to be a poorly tzu who gets better."

Maisie was worried now, all of a sudden she thought she had taken on a bigger task than she thought she was ready for, but there was no way she was going to back down now. She was brave as a lion, just like Stanley and Paddy, and this was her moment.

She went in to the girls' room to see a very tiny tzu tucked up in the enormous bed. She remembered when she had awoken in that same bed on her first morning in Tzu Kingdom although she didn't remember it being that big and she was sure she hadn't been that small.

She jumped straight up on the big bed and tapped Beth on her forehead. Beth jumped, looking frightened.

"Beth, don't worry, it's me, Maisie, one of the tzus who rescued you. It was my magic key that opened the door and brought you to safety here. Don't be scared."

She stroked Beth's furry puppy ears and soothed her until she calmed down. Being so small, Beth felt very comfortable with Maisie straight away and snuggled in to her fur, quietly sniffling to herself.

"What can I do to help you get better little Beth?" she asked.

In the quietest of whispers, right in to Maisie's long ear she told her what the problem was...

"I just want my mother."

Chapter 63

IT quite broke Maisie's heart to know that the one thing that would make Beth better was the one thing that she could not possibly deliver. But showing that she was upset too was not going to help.

'What would Coffee do?' she thought to herself as she cuddled Beth and realised that the Queen would be honest and gently tell her the truth and see what could be done to make the situation better.

She coughed, this was something she had to get just right so clearing her throat was a good start.

"Sweet Beth, I'm sorry, but that is the one thing that no one can do for you. Your mother died saving you and left you in safe paws with Phoebe and all of us."

Beth sniffled and replied, "I know, but I miss her and Phoebe is so big and strong that I am a bit scared of her. I like you because you are little like me."

"Don't you worry about Phoebe being big! She is one of the sweetest, kindest and bravest tzus I know and she will be a wonderful adoptive mother for you. Plus, there's loads of other tzus who will look after you. A few weeks ago, I was ill and weak and they rescued me too — Phoebe is a good friend of mine now and you have to cherish her because your mother entrusted her to look after you in the tzu way, until you are strong enough to find a human family to love you."

Maisie explained more about her journey and all about

her wonderful home with Fleur and her family, as well as telling her about the friends that she had in Tzu Kingdom and her amazing boyfriend Stanley.

In the next bed, one of the mother tzus, who was still confined to quarters, stirred and said hello to Maisie. Beth hid her head under the cover at the sound of another.

"Beth...what's the matter? Are you frightened of speaking?"

"I just don't know what to say," she answered, embarrassed. Maisie laughed too, that's something she had never suffered from herself. Then, she had a brilliant idea and jumped down off the bed to get someone she knew would help.

"Beth this is Millicent. You don't need to speak to anyone but her now. Just say what you want to say into her fur and she will pass on whatever you say to whomever you say it!"

Beth looked at the pink bear and smiled broadly.

"She smells nice" she said.

"Hello bed neighbour," she said in to pink fur. The tzu in the next bed waved "yoo hoo".

Beth giggled and sniffed in the air as a waft of Mabel and Myrtle's soup making filled the room.

"Do you want some soup?" Maisie asked, sensing that she was a little better now she could communicate and was delighted when Beth smiled back and nodded.

"Who does Millicent belong to Maisie?" she enquired.

"Well," said a very grown up Maisie, "she was my teddy bear, Stanley rescued her for me and I love her of course but, now, she's your bear because you need her the most."

Chapter 64

THE evening of the party had finally arrived and Stanley burped on his arrival into the Welcome Room, wearing the new red tie that Mama had bought him for being good at a business meeting they went to. He reflected on just how much had happened since the last one, just days after Queen Coffee had invited him to Tzu Kingdom on that cold and snowy day in his garden.

He had loads of tzu friends now, just like he had wished for, he had been involved in three rescues, so he knew for sure he was as brave as a lion, and a girlfriend called Maisie, who was more than he could ever have dreamed of. As he thought happy thoughts about her, he heard a little cough and there she was with Nancy — both of them looking absolutely stunning.

"Wowsers! You both look beautiful!" he said as Maisie jumped up and kissed his nose.

"Evening lovely ladies..." came a gruff voice from behind him. It was Paddy with Phoebe and they were holding paws, which pleased Stanley immensely. Paddy was smiling from ear to ear as he winked at Stan and looked up to his Feebs.

There was something Paddy wasn't saying, thought Stanley. Apart from the massive grin, which could be explained away by the fact that he was now officially Phoebe's boyfriend, Paddy's eyes were wide as saucers and he was humming to himself subconsciously.

"What you up to Paddy? You look like the dog who got the sausages!"

"Me? Nothing." he said innocently, well, at least trying to be. "Nothing. Nothing whatsoever. Nope. Nowt."

Phoebe laughed "There's going to be a few announcements later on...we are not allowed to say any more than that because we promised Coffee and Bailey."

"Well I hope these announcements are made early because Paddy here is fit to burst!" laughed Nancy.

The friends went in to the Party Room and grabbed a booth where they were joined by Bonnie and Colin.

Phoebe was over the moon to report that Beth was looking a little better now, was eating well and had even been out of bed a couple of times and ventured out to see the other puppies too. Of course, the newly named jewel and metal pups were too young for the party but, she was happy to report, all the mother and father tzus were well enough and would be coming down for the announcements and a quick snack, although they probably weren't up to a Paw Stomp just yet. Next time, they all agreed, nodding sagely.

"Oh and Maisie," said Phoebe, "I'm glad you made us rescue Millicent that night. You were right, teddy bears are important, Beth loves her." She winked and Maisie's ears pricked up proudly.

Paddy was pleased to tell his friends that the four boys, Brickie, Percy, Sammy and Hiro, would be back tonight and Maisie was tremendously excited to hear this news. They were all happy in their new homes – they'd all ended up in the Lake District – Brickie and Hiro with a family with teenagers to play with and Percy and Sammy just a few streets away with an older couple who had teenage grandchildren. They had all landed on their paws there, growing bigger and stronger with every day. Maisie was looking forward to seeing her friends.

Nancy was pleased to announce that Maisie was officially her little sister now and that everything had gone to plan. Maisie slept in Fleur's room and played with the children once Nancy had retired for the night to the Grandpops Annexe with Ifan to snooze and watch an old film. No one had claimed Maisie as theirs — they all sniggered at the mere idea of it — and so Fleur and Skye's mummy had said that they would keep her forever now. What was even better was that she had said that when Skye was a little older, she could have a shih tzu too, she just had to prove she was responsible enough and Fleur was helping her to demonstrate this.

"Honestly," said Nancy, "I genuinely don't think they will be happy until they fill that big house full of little tzus!"

"That's lovely to hear," said Bonnie and then turned to Colin, Maisie and Stanley and, with her head on one side, asked "what's the news on Tzu Gallery?"

"We are ready to launch tonight — it's all sorted and I love it," said Colin. "Stan's going to announce it at the end of the King's speech. You know, in actual fact I have found my vocation in life, I just can't imagine anything I would rather do. All the paintings of the Kings and Queens are done and I just can't wait for Bailey and Coffee to see their coronation painting. There's the Family Wall that will have all the known tzus on it and your portraits are hung already, then there's the Moments Wall with paintings of all the special and important things that have happened in Tzu Kingdom since the fairies gifted it to us. Then there's the Remember Wall and one special unveiling tonight. I just hope that Bailey finally forgives himself for my injury — I know I wanted to be a rescuer at first but now, art is my thing and I am happier than I ever thought possible. I know it was because I got injured but, well, things have a funny way of working themselves out if you have a positive attitude."

As Colin finished speaking, the music went off and King Bailey and Queen Coffee stood on the stage. It was time for some important announcements.

Chapter 65

KING Bailey spoke first and introduced his **Queen**.

"Tzus, it is wonderful to see so many of you here tonight. As you are no doubt pleased to hear, and a little excited too I'll wager, tonight will be the usual mix of merriment, food and friendship and not too much talking!"

Everyone laughed, he knew them all so well.

"But first, please say good evening to my stunning wife and your caring **Queen....Coffee.**"

The applause and wolf whistles were deafening. There wasn't anything not to love about **Queen Coffee** and tonight she looked a picture, with her long silky ears fresh out of fur curlers, her tail swishing happily whilst wearing a crocheted dress of gold and cream that really showed off her fur.

As she opened her mouth to speak, Bailey himself whistled at her and she giggled.

"Tzus, please listen carefully as there are to be a few changes at Tzu Kingdom following the events of past weeks."

There was mumbling amongst the crowd, they hoped it was nothing serious or unwelcome.

"As you know, I have been **Chief Scout** since Nancy retired some years ago but it has become apparent that a tzu cannot be **Queen** and lead the **Scout** team. Both roles need someone dedicated to one thing so, tonight, I am announcing that I will be stepping down as Lead Scout and passing the stewardship of Scout Tower and the Scout team to...PADDY."

There were whoops and cheers for popular Paddy and Stan slapped him on the back in a playful way.

"Well done mate," he said, "no wonder you were bursting to tell someone!"

"I know Stanley it's not been easy keeping that a secret since this afternoon! We'll celebrate with a steak pie in a minute!"

Queen Coffee continued.

"So that means that I can dedicate all my time to being your Queen and to King Bailey, my darling husband."

"Aww..." said the crowd, in unison.

"Of course, Paddy will need help so I am further pleased to announce that Bonnie is promoted to Scout-second-in-command with special responsibility for paperwork and filing."

Everyone cheered again, Paddy the loudest, knowing that she loved to organise things. She also had plans to work out a food diary for Paddy, but he didn't know about this yet.

"And with us being so busy now" continued the Queen "we are in need of additional scouts and therefore Paddy and Bonnie will be looking out for tzus of just the right skills and temperament to join their team."

"Now, on to the Rescuer Team. You will be aware that following the biggest rescue in our time - Bailey will say more on this later - our dear Phoebe made a promise to look after a baby tzu. Well, that tzu is now thriving in the hospital wing thanks to the Comforter Tzus and other friends but, again, we must concentrate on the most important job of the time and, therefore, Phoebe will be taking a break from being a rescuer to be a mum to little Beth."

"Aww..." said the crowd and looked over at Phoebe, who was blushing a little.

"This of course means that Tanner needs someone to fill her boots and, with these being such big boots to fill, we are temporarily promoting Kiki *and* Lola to lead rescuers and with the need for rescues so crucial these days, we are promoting Zero and Biddy to Rescuer Trainers."

Another round of applause and the tzus waved thank you.

"Bailey, I think that's all I have to say tonight." Everyone applauded and cheered as the Queen passed over to the King.

"Coffee, you forgot to mention, that you and Nancy will be leading us in a Paw Stomp to begin the evening begin with a swing...isn't it lovely to see Nancy back everyone...!"

Cheers echoed through the hall with whispers as some of the younger tzus asking the elders to tell them who Nancy was later. She waved back, confidently, loving being back in the limelight.

"Tzus....friends...it has been a busy few weeks in Tzu Kingdom. Our work is expanding as bad humans seem to be advancing but, I am pleased to say, for every bad human there are ten good ones."

A defiant round of applause erupted. "Like knowers..." whispered Paddy to Stanley "...and mums and dads and families" he whispered back.

"We have rescued a number of tzus less fortunate of late and I am pleased to see some of them here tonight including little Maisie, the six parents from the big rescue and the four brothers from the roadside. I also announce that we are expanding the rescue team and those brave young brothers Percy, Sammy, Brickie and Hiro have, tonight, volunteered to be trained as rescuers."

"Bravo! Lion Brave! Good boys!" shouted out tzus from the crowd.

"What with Paddy's plans for expanding the Scout team, it looks like now Queen Coffee is full time ruling with me, we will be looking for new Welcomers and Comforters too before long!"

The tzus all started to discuss what they would like to apply for and a noisy hub bub filled the room. Bailey called the room to order.

"There is just one sad thing to announce, although I am sure all are aware, but we did lose a tzu-less-fortunate at the Big Rescue. We shall never forget Molly so we will be looking to make a permanent memorial to brave young Molly in the fullness of time.

Down in the crowd, someone was being nudged. "Stan, Stan...now," said Colin. Stan felt awfully nervous about interrupting the King this time. He'd been quite willing to put his paw in the air at the last party when he didn't know anyone but now, in from of a room of tzus who knew who he was, he felt all embarrassed.

"AHEM AHEM!" coughed Colin and Maisie making others turn around so that Stan had no option but to raise his paw.

"Yes Stanley?" said King Bailey.

"Erm, well, the thing is King Bailey," he said, feeling all hot and prickly, "Colin, Maisie and I have been working on something special and, well, we would like to show you what that is..."

Maisie had quickly made her way, with Colin, to the black curtains.

"Please look to the back of the hall," said Stanley as Colin pulled the curtains open and Maisie produced the key.

"Follow me." she said as she unlocked the big door and pushed it open.

Chapter 66

BAILEY and Coffee walked through to the revamped Tzu Gallery and gasped as they admired the portraits of the Kings and Queens.

They thought the portrait of King Leo was stunning and showed what a special tzu he was. They paused at King Wolfgang, wondering whatever did happen to the King of Peace. Queen Sally's portrait was vague, they knew little about her as she had ruled for such a short time, then playboy Romeo, the founder of Scout Tower, they laughed at the posing rock star brother kings Groovy, Elvis and Bolan who had ruled one after the other during some of the most colourful years and then smiled at Muffin, a most serious of rulers. They admired the flowery portrait of Queen Gypsophillia, then Hamish and finally Mirabelle and then her son, their dear friend Pierre.

They were not prepared for the next portrait of themselves and all the tzus noticed that they squeezed each other's paws.

"Colin. Stanley. Maisie." said the King sternly, come hither my children.

This was very formal they thought, hoping they weren't in trouble.

He stood before them and every tzu in the room held their breath.

"Thank you, we love it, we love you too."

He flung his paws open and they all ran to him and Coffee for the biggest of hugs as everyone cheered.

"Do you really love it Bailey and Coffee?" asked Maisie.

"We do, we think it is wonderful. I don't even remember why I locked it up now. We should celebrate our reign because of our pride in everyone in Tzu Kingdom."

"Exactly!" said Colin, winking at Stanley and knowing that their plan had worked.

"We would like to show you a special picture, especially for Coffee" an excited Maisie blurted out. They removed a large sheet and revealed a painted copy of Coffee and Bailey's wedding photo. Coffee was speechless as the wedding party of Bailey and her, Franc, Centime and dear Nancy shone out.

They showed them the Family Wall where all the current tzu paintings would hang which had, for now, about a dozen pictures of current tzus, then they showed him the rest of the Moments Wall where all the pictures of important events and fun times would hang and then, finally, the Remember Wall, where all the pictures from the Family Wall would move one day, so they could be remembered after they had closed their eyes for the last time.

"King Bailey and Queen Coffee," said Colin, "would you like to unveil the one painting that currently resides upon the Remember Wall."

They nodded and Stan led them to a cord which they put their paws on and pulled down together. It unveiled a stunning painting of Molly lying comfortably on a cloud amongst the moon and stars, looking down on young Beth for all time.

Coffee wiped her tears and then passed her handkerchief to Bailey.

"It's beautiful Colin, you are quite the artist." she asserted.

"We shall always remember her this way," said Bailey,

"but, tzus, I do believe Molly wanted her daughter and, indeed, all of us to live our lives well in her memory. So I think it's time for us all to enjoy a Paw Stomp...let's get our boots on!"

Chapter 67

THE Paw Stomp was one of the loudest that had ever been danced! Peekaboo was back to call the moves and with Coffee dancing with Nancy, Colin danced with Bailey whilst Phoebe and Paddy danced together and Stanley showed off his best moves to Maisie.

'STOMP STOMP STOMP STOMP' it went and, just like before, a heap of exhausted tzus collapsed on the floor as it got faster and faster around the floor until in the end, Franc and Centime were the only ones left standing!

The laughter was infectious and, as they headed to the buffet, the giggles didn't die down a bit.

Colin had found himself very busy after the launch of Tzu Gallery as he had a steady stream of tzus asking him to sketch them for the Family Wall. He didn't mind, he loved it, and Coffee and Bailey looked on happily, knowing that this was what Colin wanted to do.

Stanley and Paddy found themselves sat at the bar together watching the others dance whilst they had a drink.

"So, Stan the man, I got my wish," said Paddy, "I'm Chief Scout...YIKES!"

"You've done brilliantly Pads, I am especially proud of you" said Stan, truthfully.

"Thanks Stan, but, well, the thing is, I am only as

good as the tzus around me and, well, Bonnie has her skills, but I think I need all my besties around me, so I was just wondering, I know they want you to train for a rescuer position, s I would understand if you said no, but well, would you work with me as Scout Leader's Assistant?"

Working with Paddy? Being a scout? Stanley thought about it for a second and, as much as being a rescuer would be very exciting and heroic, he liked being high up in Scout Tower with Paddy and finding those less fortunate and, to be honest, he'd done quite a lot of rescuing in his short time in Tzu Kingdom and he didn't know he wanted to make a career out of it. He loved his other life too with Mama and Daddy and he wanted to be sure he would always be as safe as he could when he was out of their sight.

"Paddy I would be honoured to be your assistant!" he said, doing a little happy dance on his stool!

Chapter 68

THE party was coming to an end with a slow Shih Tzu Shuffle underway on the dance floor. Stanley and Maisie were dancing together, right next to the King and Queen. Paddy and Phoebe had just gone up to Scout Tower to check things before home time. Colin had closed his etching queue for the night, saying he had plenty to keep him busy for now and was dancing with Bonnie.

The lights went up in the main hall as the dancing finished and, as before, the tzus broke in to tidy teams to ensure the Kingdom was tidy for the morning, just like they had promised the fairies.

Stanley was tidying with Maisie, Bonnie and Colin when the familiar sound of fast running paw steps came from above and got louder and louder as they got nearer and nearer.

It was Paddy. He collapsed by the bar and caught his breath.

"What is it Paddy?" said Coffee.

"I've just been up Scout Tower QC and..." he wheezed "there's some baby tzus...and they're in mortal peril...."

"Here we go again!" exclaimed Stanley, "brave as a lion time!"

Book Two:

The Tzu King Mystery

PADDY Boo the Shih Tzu scout was shaken up and the tzus gathered around him on his bar stool to hear his latest tale.

His friend Stanley was more than familiar with his funny and over-dramatic ways but he accepted them, because that's what friends do.

It had been the end of a great party in Tzu Kingdom, at which King Bailey and Queen Coffee had announced Paddy would be promoted to Chief Scout now that Coffee would be concentrating on her regal duties. It was fitting, somehow, that his first shift in full charge of Scout Tower had resulted in him finding tzus in peril that desperately needed rescuing. Paddy did tend to embellish his stories but, Stan mused, he certainly did look worried, even for him.

As usual, the tzus who kept the bar gave him a glass of milk to steady his nerves as he began to reveal what he had seen through the Scout Tower telescopes...

"Well, Feebs and I were up there just having a final look before we went to say goodnight to puppy Beth and tuck her in when I just heard some crying. I scanned around where I heard it from and there.... just inside the door of an abandoned building by a harbour wall I saw them..one boy at first... obviously the one in charge....and then.....four more puppies... in a...a...box."

The tzus in the party room gasped. Already, they knew those puppies were in a bad situation, a situation with no love. As more often than not, he was right. Something had to be done.

At that point, Phoebe, Paddy's girlfriend stood beside him. She had returned from the Comforter Wing where she had bedded down and given a goodnight kiss to her adopted puppy Beth, an orphan from another rescue some weeks earlier who now, thankfully, was already starting to look much better in the care of the comforter tzus and a teddy bear called Millicent who had recently been rescued with a tzu-in-peril, now called Maisie and a regular visitor to the Kingdom from the fairy door at her new home, where she had a princess bed and a family to love her.

"Thank goodness they have each other," said Phoebe, as she took Paddy's free paw, "but, we only have a day or so to rescue them and bring them to safety before they end up in an even worse situation. Looking at it from a rescuer tzu perspective and where they are, the safest place for the rescue would actually be on the high seas but...."

"....that's where it gets really tricky..." interjected Paddy as he took up the story, "...it's a watery rescue."

Wise King Bailey of Tzus walked over to the pair and tapped Paddy on the shoulder with a smile.

"Paddy," he said, "it's been a while since we did a sea rescue but we have experience — Tanner has led them before so we will just get the salty sea books up from the vault and plan it together. It's all going to be ok, we just need to be prepared!"

Paddy looked up at his King, his eyes bloodshot and his brow furrowed.

"No KB, I don't think you quite understand. It's not a sea rescue itself that's such a worry but *where* it is...."

The King looked at him blankly for a second and turned to Coffee for her advice. She mouthed a word to him and he shook himself into seriousness.

"Oh my dogness, you don't mean that the sea rescue will have to take place at the place that we don't bark of, not there, please...tell me it isn't so?"

Paddy nodded and rubbed his eyes. Stanley took little Maisie's paw and they drew closer, intrigued.

"Paddy, Phoebe," said Queen Coffee, almost frozen to the spot with fear "you can't, well, surely not there? Not the place that is only known to royalty, senior rescuers and Chief Scouts?"

The look on Paddy's face said it all. Phoebe stifled a sniff. Stan and Maisie looked at each other with wide eyes.

Nancy, Maisie's newfound older sister and the Queen's oldest friend, piped up. "Not there. Not the very place where a former ruler went on a rescue and was never heard from again?"

Phoebe replied, "yes, the most scary place ever known to any tzu who has ever passed through the fairy doors".

Stanley and Maisie could take no more — they were both scared but excited and, more than anything, they wanted to know what the elders and the tzus-of-experience were all talking about.

"What is this place that we don't bark of, that is only known to royalty and senior rescuers and chief scouts, that is terribly scary and is where a former ruler disappeared to never be heard from again?" enquired an agitated Stanley.

"WHERE?" shouted Maisie, stomping her paw.

Together, all those in the know turned to the young pair and put a name to the most terrifying place in Tzu Kingdom.

"WOLFGANG WATERS."

To keep up to date with all things Tzu Kingdom

please visit www.tzukingdom.com

Find Tzu Kingdom on Twitter and Facebook too.

About the Authors

Karen Chilvers was born in Essex in 1971 and lives in Warley, Brentwood. Pets have been an important feature in her life and she's had five cats (Yogi, Boo Boo, Schnapps, Dillon and Daisy) and six dogs (Cherie, Nancy, Gypsy, Quincy, Louis and King Bailey) in her life. She's single. She's cool with that.

Gill Eastgate was born in Edinburgh in 1971, as a child she wanted a pony but ended up with a rabbit. Stanley is her first dog who has since, quite simply changed her life. She lives in the suburbs of Edinburgh with Stan and her husband Ray, who is affectionately referred to as the 'Tzu Father' due to his 'tzu-like' beard.

©Barking Cat Pet Photography

Acknowledgments

Karen would like to thank Vikki Kavanagh for constantly telling her she could write for twenty years and to be an author. Her mum for being there always, her sister for giving her someone to have a wild imagination for her in her youth but, most of all, the Shih Tzus in her life Quincy, Louis and Bailey.

Gill would like to thank the wonderful world of Twitter, after all without it, Karen and Gill would never have met. Her mum just for being her mum, her husband Ray for listening intently to the happenings in Tzu Kingdom without thinking she was completely mad, her wonderful Shih Tzu Stanley, and of course her much loved and sadly missed Dad.

Karen and Gill both wish to thank actor Callum Hughes for voicing Stanley in the short film "Stanley's Secret", Michelle Smith at ToonPetz.com for the beautiful Shih Tzu illustrations, Britain's Next Bestseller for the opportunity to publish their first book and all the fur-friends across the world that have supported us and made us laugh and cry over the years.